SEVEN DAYS IN AUGUST

BRIT BILDØEN

SEVEN DAYS IN AUGUST

TRANSLATED BY BECKY L. CROOK

LONDON NEW YORK CALCUTTA

Seagull Books, 2022

Originally published in Norwegian as *Sju dagar i august*
© Brit Bildøen, 2014
Published in agreement with Stilton Literary Agency

First published in English translation by Seagull Books, 2016
English Translation © Becky L. Crook, 2016

This translation has been published with the financial
support of NORLA

ISBN 978 0 8574 2 382 5

British Library Cataloguing-in-Publication Data
A catalogue record for this book is available from
the British Library

Typeset by Seagull Books, Calcutta, India
Printed and bound by WordWorth India, New Delhi, India

THURSDAY

Sofie was studying the living room through a green-stemmed glass when Otto called from the kitchen. He wanted her to set the table. Otto preferred the normal, plain glasses, he thought the green ones were too small, but Sofie enjoyed taking out the old, inherited set. The glasses looked handsome on the table, the wine tasted different in them, somehow. Each sip was more precious. The living room bulged green through the wine glass. She nearly lost her balance, and set the glass down. Otto called again.

'All right!' she replied.

They pulled out their chairs in unison. Otto had arranged cod and mashed potatoes on the plates, with stripes of pickled peppers running like scars down the fillets. The fish white as porcelain, the potatoes crammed with yellow butter.

'When does it start?' asked Otto.

'Eight,' said Sofie. 'But I don't at all feel up to it.'

'Up to it? It's not really about that, is it?'

'No, I suppose I must go.'

'Must you or mustn't you go?'

'I must.'

'You know, I don't really want to go either.'

'It would be taken as an act of protest if I *didn't* attend.'

Sofie poked her fork in the potatoes, pulled herself together and brought the food to her mouth.

'What is that on your arm?'

Sofie looked questioningly at Otto. She looked down. She was wearing a wide wooden armband on her left wrist. She pushed it upwards.

'Oh, that's just some insect bite.'

'It's not a tick bite, is it? It doesn't look very good. Maybe you should have it checked out.'

'It only looks like that because I've been scratching at it. I cleaned it, the swelling will soon go down.'

Otto sighed, but didn't say more. A rattling sound echoed from downstairs on the street.

The veranda door was cracked open, allowing air and noise to filter in. Dust from the street accompanied the air, leaving behind a thin, grey film on top of picture frames and books. But this was something he appreciated, that there wasn't an airtight barrier separating their life among those white, art-filled walls from the colourful life on the streets below. Two years after moving in, they'd bought and refurbished the attic as well. Otto could still feel the project like a jovial reverberation in his muscles. He and Sofie usually said that they had chosen this neighbourhood because it was lively, and because all kinds of people lived there. Others would say it was multicultural but Otto was cautious about using words like that. He was annoyed that Sofie often used an expression she'd gleaned from a wealthy lady at some exhibit or other: 'society's crown'. Since she didn't bother explaining what it meant, people rarely understood her joke. There were a lot of people who didn't think Sofie knew how to joke at all. What the wealthy lady meant by her quip was that she herself had landed among the upper 'boughs' of society, the 'crown' of the tree. She characterized herself as one of the privileged. 'Here where we live, up high in the loftiest branches, with views above city rooftops, we are aware that we're among the privileged on *society's crown*,' Sofie would say when they gave their guests a tour. And sometimes she would add: 'If we were still on the west side, we would feel closer to the trunk.' She never noticed the questioning glances directed her way when she said things like this. But Otto noticed them.

'It seems like there's more traffic these days,' said Sofie.

'A lot of it is rerouted traffic. It will get better once they've finished the new block.'

'The Grove. Haven't you heard that they are calling it The Grove? There's no longer such a thing as a blockhouse or flats. Now they are all referred to as something like The Grove, and Garden Homes and Townhouses.'

'Whatever,' said Otto, shrugging.

5

Sofie went to change into one of the dresses she wore for exhibition openings. Otto followed her upstairs to change his shirt. She was standing in front of the open closet, studying the row of black dresses. How many did she have? What were the factors she used in deciding which to wear? To Otto, all of the dresses appeared identical.

'You feel that you have to go because of Karin,' he said, zipping her up in the back. He liked the way she held up her hair so it wouldn't catch in the zipper. A dry aroma wafted from her neck. Sun-warmed stone.

'Well, it is in fact my department! But yes, this secret opening was Karin's idea. Though it isn't a secret, actually. Everyone believes they've received an exclusive invitation, or that they're on the guest list because of someone they know. They're going to revolt when they figure out that absolutely everyone else is there, too.'

'Then at least I can look forward to watching all of their faces as they come in.'

'The photographs are wonderful,' said Sofie, 'and some of the videos are actually so . . . '

'I probably won't be able to see anything through the crowds,' interrupted Otto.

He went down to the kitchen to make coffee. His glasses fogged up as he blew into his cup.

'Depp will be playing.' Sofie pulled out the stool beside him.

'And you're only just telling me now?'

'Another one of her notions,' Sofie mumbled into her coffee cup. He had chosen the yellow mocha cups.

'That's unbelievable! You haven't exactly been touting this evening, but it sounds terrific. What about the artist herself? She's a real wildcat. Will there be any scandals?'

'You're thinking of the time she . . .

'Bit the cultural minister!' he laughed. 'Talk about biting the hand that feeds you.'

Sofie shook her head slowly. Otto studied her.

'It isn't . . . are you afraid it will be a success, is that it? That Karin will gain an upper hand?'

She sent him a challenging look. 'Karin can have as much success as she wants, as long as she doesn't use it to pressure me. That's what I'm afraid of. I am so tired of intrigue, so terribly sick of it!'

Otto patted her on the back. Sofie pushed his hand away.

'We should get going.'

The stairwell was dark in places. The tenants rarely got around to replacing the light bulbs, although they were officially under obligation to do it on their own floors. Otto took a large sidestep around a bag of rubbish outside a door one storey below theirs. Sofie couldn't restrain herself and gave the bag a little kick. Coffee grounds spilt from the bag onto the doormat.

'Good job with that one,' said Otto.

They were short on time and decided to cycle. But Sofie soon realized that her dress was not the most practical cycling outfit. It was a bit too short, but since the ride to the museum was mostly down-hill, she decided to try pedalling with her knees clasped demurely together.

Seven years earlier, when they had moved into Jens Bjelkes Gata, her workplace had been only a three-minute walk away. She'd started working at the museum around the same time that they'd moved to the Tøyen neighbourhood, before the museum had picked up and moved to Bjørvika. Which felt like a long time ago, like another life. It *was* another life. Over the years, the area had changed but it was hard to put a finger on exactly what it was that had changed. Perhaps they were the ones who had begun viewing things differently. The area had always been somewhat run-down, and it wasn't a new thing, really, that paper and plastic tumbled in circles down the street, that people drove wildly or jaywalked without looking. She was always on alert as she cycled down along Tøyengata. For good reason—here was someone stepping out in front of her right now. Sofie pulled hard on the brakes, and the back wheel emitted a squeaking noise. A lanky, young man in a red T-shirt shot her a frightened look which quickly shifted to another expression. He mumbled something, a growl from deep at the back of his throat. He pushed his chin out and banged his hands down on her handlebars. Then he continued walking.

Both of Sofie's feet were planted on the ground, and now they began to tremble. A group of men who had been talking loudly had gone quiet and stood, looking at her. There was something in their faces, something expectant, Sofie didn't know how to decipher their expressions. She pushed up with one foot and kicked ahead with the other, managed to shove off and continue riding. Otto hadn't seen any of it, he had already crossed the intersection where she had stopped. She could barely see his back far down the street.

By the time she reached him, he was waiting at the bridge.

'Is your dress slowing you down?'

'No, it's these damn people who walk straight out into the street, like they have an invisible red carpet rolled in front of them wherever they go. I almost hit one of them, and this wasn't the first time.'

'Ah.'

'The dress,' she said, her voice breaking. 'The dress is really the least of my problems.'

'I'm sorry I didn't wait for you,' said Otto.

She inhaled deeply. 'It's all right.' She looked at her watch. 'It's eight now.'

'We're nearly there,' he said.

The museum's glass facade looked leaden in the humid autumn evening. Viewed from the bridge, the building seemed to lean out over the water. As they drew closer, it nearly straightened up again. A banner was strung across the entrance, the letters in earth tones. One had to be close up to read what it said. GLOOMY NORWAY. Followed by the name of the artist, Jenny Wegelmann. This was the first of several exhibits for which Norwegian artists were commissioned to expand upon the motifs in Edvard Munch's art. Jenny Wegelmann delved into bleakness and darkness. Melancholy. Twilight. She was a photographer and her work portrayed snapshots of barren, snow-covered forest roads, sometimes with tracks from people or vehicles. Her videos were shot in park alleyways at daybreak, with one or two figures rushing past, their features a blur. It was gloomy, so it worked. The jury had loved it.

Sofie liked this exhibition, but was sceptical about the concept itself. The first series of exhibitions was entitled 'Melancholy in Our Times'. Shallow, thought Sofie. Too easy. Superficial. Embarrassing, actually, to issue such a call to Norwegian artists. But she was the only one in the organization to ask these critical questions, and in the last few days the interest from Norwegian and foreign journalists was incredible.

And it was all up to Karin now, anyway. They spotted her as they entered. An exclamation mark in a red frock. Everything on Karin's body seemed to stand upright, her cheekbones, her shoulders, her hips, her brown knees protruding beneath her dress. She was skinny without looking gaunt, and now she was manoeuvring towards them with agile movements, both arms outstretched. She kissed Sofie on both cheeks, as though they didn't see each other every single day. Otto received the same treatment, and an additional compliment:

'Fabulous shirt!'

'Thanks. Of course, it was Sofie who . . . '

His shirt was pale blue, almost silver. But Karin's attention had wandered away and further out into the public. She stood, nervously shifting her weight from foot to foot. There was something Otto had said about her, Sofie didn't recall precisely, but she hadn't forgotten it either. Something about how she was beautiful and cheeky the way that only girls from Bergen could be. Sofie had never been jealous of Karin, she didn't think Otto was attracted to her in that way even if he had praised her high cheekbones on more than one occasion. Irritatingly high, thought Sofie now; she could see that Karin had highlighted them with a thick layer of rouge.

'Well, Karin. Everyone is here!'

'Yes, it really exceeds our expectations!' Karin blew them both a kiss and vanished. Sofie watched her depart. A guest in her own home. She didn't know if she said this aloud or merely thought it. Otto greeted some journalists who stood in a cluster. One of them waved limply with his hand. He was probably trying to appear nonchalant. Bordering on weary.

'The young dead,' mumbled Otto.

'The aged youth. Isn't this the generation that's supposed to represent the new authenticity?'

'Well, an authentic fatigue at any rate.'

'They've figured it out.'

'What?'

'That Karin has hoodwinked them.'

'Well, they don't exactly look worked up about it.'

Sofie felt at once exhausted to her marrow. The human wall looked impenetrable. The din of voices echoed sharply in the new, sterile hall. Thankfully, there was a small outcropping where a young woman was serving sparkling wine. The first sip tickled Sofie's nose. And suddenly a warm, clammy hand touched her bare arm.

'Hi, boss.'

It was Aasmund in his chequered shirt. Always chequered, long-sleeved shirts, regardless of the occasion. He was one of the curators with whom she had the best connection. And, besides being a jokester, he was one of the only people working in the museum who hadn't suddenly changed his behaviour towards her when she had been appointed head of the department responsible for the organization of exhibitions and collections. Even now, months later, people continued to dramatize her promotion. Sofie suspected that all of their comments and encouragements were sarcastic. But Aasmund was one of the few people who would look you in the eye. Sofie couldn't think of anything to say at the moment so she merely nodded and raised her glass.

'Well, everyone is certainly happy.' Aasmund made a sweeping gesture around the room.

'Really? Well, then, we should be happy too.'

Aasmund brought his glass to hers, clinked them lightly together and blinked.

'For Edvard.'

'For Edvard,' she replied seriously. He's on my side, she thought, but doubted it just as quickly.

'Even the cultural minister seems to be in a good mood.'

'The cultural minister? Is the cultural minister here?'

Aasmund nodded and pointed. Sofie didn't see him at first, but she saw Otto's back as he milled about by himself, perusing the exhibit. She hadn't even noticed that he had left her side. He stood before an enormous photograph of a stack of logs piled near a snow-covered forest road. The cut surfaces of the logs illuminated the photo in a way that made the snow appear grey. Do trees really contain so much light? Otto thought about the case documents waiting for him at home, the damned Ullern case. He was longing to be done with it, or at least to be able to gain an overview. But these cases were never really finished. He exchanged short nods with the cultural minister as they passed each other. Sofie hadn't mentioned that he would be at the opening. Otto turned to look for his wife. She was still talking with her colleague, the one whose name he couldn't remember. Was it Asgeir? Aasgeir? Sofie looked so small beside him. She stood there twisting her bracelet. It was so typical of her to fiddle with her jewellery when she was nervous. Otto was usually annoyed over how she twisted her wedding ring whenever she spoke to people. As if she were trying to screw herself into the ground.

Sofie realized she was scratching the bite under her bracelet. Aasmund also noticed.

'Mosquito bite?' he asked.

She started to say something, but stopped herself. She just nodded and attempted to position the bracelet on her wrist so that it wouldn't rub against the bite. Had Karin invited the cultural minister without informing her? Was he planning to say something? The official opening would not take place until tomorrow. Sofie kept Karin in her sights.

She shifted smoothly through the crowd, a red thread drawing together the various groups. Karin must have noticed her gaze, for she abruptly set course for the safe zone that Sofie had established on the periphery with Aasmund. Sofie began twisting her bracelet again.

Karin leant in close to Sofie's ear.

'About the cultural minister . . . '

'I didn't realize he would be coming.'

'Neither did I, until this afternoon. But if he asks to say a few words . . . '

Sofie wrinkled her forehead but nodded, and soon Karin was standing up on the white, portable podium that seemed to hover slightly above the ground like a magic carpet. Karin began abruptly, without any coughing or tapping of the microphone. Sofie heard the crowd's friendly murmur, and thought of the first performance review they'd had after her appointment as new department head. Karin had expressed her exuberance at being able to work directly with the exhibitions and public, which made it tricky afterwards for Sofie to address the tension between them. She knew that Karin had felt slighted. And she also knew that most of those who'd been working at the museum for a while were of the opinion that Karin's long years of service should have outweighed Sofie's research work and lengthy list of publications.

'And, as a surprise, the cultural minister now wishes to come and share a few words,' Karin concluded, stepping aside. Bearing a bouquet of long, dark-red gladioli, the cultural minister lost his balance as he headed up the podium. Karin quickly liberated him from the flowers.

'Yes, it certainly is surprising that I would dare show up to greet this artist after what happened between her and my predecessor,' the minister began, amid laughter and hoots from the audience. 'But because this is a special occasion, I'll take the chance,' he continued, blinking nervously and removing a note from the inner pocket of his grey suit. Sofie thought he looked somewhat like a flower himself, he reminded her mostly of a tulip, alone in a glass vase—thin body, heavy, tilted head. His speech made her happy. It wasn't the typical ministerial speech, an attempt to take credit for the museum's existence but, rather, a speech about the heritage of Munch, which had often been viewed as too heavy a burden for such a small country and such a small capital city to bear. 'We, and by that I mean, first and foremost, politicians,' said the cultural minister, 'have had a tendency to see problems, and not opportunities. We see the costs before we see something of value. But look,' he pointed around him, 'look at what this important artist has influenced, how he has inspired and shaped, not only generations of artists, but also us as a people, enabling us to create a timeless impression of our way of life, of the living conditions of these peculiar people who live so far north: the cold, the illnesses, the struggles—but also the sun, the summer light, the light in the snow, the light at night, the light on our faces,' said the cultural minister, and the public had fallen silent, people stood looking around them, Wegelmann's photographs glowed and shimmered on the surrounding walls. Sofie threw a side glance at Aasmund, who was drumming on his wine glass. He caught her gaze and nodded slowly.

Then Jenny Wegelmann came up onto the podium. Her white hair straggling as usual in every which way, her leather jacket, which was also white, and her eyes, which were so heavily made up that they appeared as two black pools on her pale face. She didn't exactly appear harmless. And the audience was given more of a treat than they had hoped for. The bouquet was once again handed to the cultural minister, who had to bend over to hand them to the artist, since he was an entire head taller than she. And as he bent, she grabbed his head in both her hands and gave him a kiss on the mouth, a long, ardent kiss. Because he was holding the bouquet with both hands, he couldn't do anything other than use it to push her away. Thus, in the cultural minister's attempt to escape Jenny Wegelmann's grip, it appeared as though he was trying to gouge her eyes out with gladioli. A camera flashed, illuminating their faces. The cultural minister scurried off the podium and the artist hid her face behind the flowers. Several of the gladioli had snapped in the scuffle.

17

Sofie pushed her way through the uproarious crowd, hoping to find the cultural minister and beg forgiveness, to put things right. Thank him for the outstanding speech, which the tiny artistic rebel had unfortunately now ensured that no one would remember. But he was already on his way out the door together with another man in a suit. Sofie almost ploughed over one of his communications officers, a young woman whose name she couldn't recall and who now stood arguing with a reporter.

'An incredibly cheap PR trick,' she lashed out in Sofie's direction. And then turned again towards the journalist. 'You shouldn't let yourselves be exploited in this way . . . this is purely a publicity stunt!'

The journalist cast the communications officer a haughty look and then glanced down at his mobile phone. 'And a successful one at that. It's already online,' he said and walked towards the door.

Sofie watched as a black car drove up outside, swallowing the cultural minister. She threw up her arms: 'Well, he came here on his own initiative.'

The woman looked at her in astonishment for a moment, then pursed her lips, turned on her heel and followed the minister. Sofie shivered, hugged her arms, though it wasn't cold. She returned to the hall. Three girls dressed in black were on the podium rigging up keyboards, guitar and bass. Next to them, Karin stood in a small cluster with

Jenny Wegelmann, the chairman of the jury and a few journalists.

Otto watched Sofie approach from the other side of the stage. She was so enigmatically beautiful, with that little half-smile behind which she always hid. A Raphaelesque paragon, Karin had called her. She was heading towards him, but then Depp started in on the first of their dark, tenacious songs and the crowd thickened around the podium. The band specialized in playing hit covers so slowly that they all sounded nearly the same. At least they all sounded equally depressing. Otto looked over at Karin and gave her a thumbs-up gesture. She flashed him a radiant smile. Apparently, it was her evening.

Sofie didn't feel like elbowing her way through the crowd, so she turned instead and made a beeline towards the back of the room, to the table with drinks. The girl serving drinks had left and she couldn't spot Aasmund anywhere. The sparkling wine had gone flat. The music sounded woolly from a distance, like vibrations from inside empty barrels. For those in attendance, it had been a fantastic performance. Sofie knew that Karin, and the rest of her staff, would conclude that the museum couldn't have had a better launch for their new endeavours. A scandalous kiss, an artist gone wild, a humiliated minister, the front page on the few remaining print newspapers. Was she the only one who found it all undignified? Sofie felt the familiar ache in her lower back, the tingling down her hips. An old pain awak-ened. Her body threatening to lock down. There was something about this opening that vexed her. That forceful, siphoning kiss. A vampire kiss.

She turned her back to the party, dug for the key card in her purse and let herself further into the museum. The escalator was off, so she took the lift and exited at the exhibition hall on the eighth floor. It was like entering a box, void of sounds and impressions. Sofie wandered slowly through the rooms without stopping at a single painting. She viewed them in a way she had never seen them before; they rolled past in a stream of colours and flashes, fragments of life's catastrophes. Scratchy coughs, short breaths, eyes bright with fever. Pale skin and elegant gowns that could only temporarily conceal the breakdown, the decomposition, smell of death. Beauty and truth in one and the same painting, in each painting, that's the important thing, thought Sofie, and continued to walk. Beauty and truth can be the same thing, that's when it becomes art. This is what we are working with, it's important to hold onto that, she thought to herself as she walked through the rooms, forgetting about time, forgetting the discomfort of that kiss for a while.

She tried to explain it to Otto on the way home. They were walking, pushing the bicycles. It wasn't quite dark yet, but the street lamps had been lit and were holding up the heavy, blue-black sky like a tent suspended overhead. The street behind the police station was nearly empty. Sofie rarely chose this route when she walked alone.

'Everything is just so . . . flat. When the thing that matters is constantly shadowed by scandals and celebrities and being hip. The minister tried to say something substantial about the art, and then . . . well, it was the artist herself who sabotaged it . . . it's just unbelievable!'

'It's still true that any publicity is good publicity.'

'But at what price? To always sensationalize everything, make everything trivial and tabloid-worthy, up for grabs by the basest of instincts? We'll never break free of being mediocre. And why? Because no one wants to break free from it. Not even the people who work with one of the greatest artists who ever lived, want to break free. Everyone is scared to death of being labelled an elitist. It's like the worst . . . '

'You're biased by your work conditions,' said Otto. 'You see everything in that light.'

'Most likely.'

'Karin and the others probably think that this little scandal will benefit the museum. But just let it go. Choose your battles!'

'And that's coming from you.'

'What do you mean?'

'No, I just mean that you seem willing enough to enter into each battle yourself. Big or small. Like the Ullern case.'

'That is, in fact, a very difficult case.'

'You see.'

His sigh. Above the sound of their steps, the light brushing of his suit jacket against the bicycle bell, the rumbling of the bus through the Grønland neighbourhood. A sigh like that indicated that the conversation was over. It meant that he felt he hadn't got anywhere with her. He heard his own sigh, too, and regretted it at once. They'd had countless discussions about this sigh.

'But, by all means,' he hurried on to say, 'you're the one at the forefront. I can understand that it must be annoying.'

She didn't reply. They passed the Indian restaurant that had been their local haunt in those first years. It had been closed for a while now but the tablecloths still decked the tables and the small vases of plastic flowers were arranged just as they had always been. Otto hoped that the friendly owner hadn't gone bankrupt. They had promised each other to make it a point to frequent the restaurant more often if it ever re-opened. Sofie passed the windows now without looking in. The name of the restaurant, appliquéd in gold, arched letters on the windowpane, was almost illegible from traffic dust.

'I hope a nice restaurant opens up soon in the neighbourhood,' said Otto to her neck. 'If only they would close The Good Neighbour and make it into a cosy little bistro!'

There tended to be a lot of noise and commotion in and around the corner pub. Now it looked quiet, but Poor Dog lay outside as usual. That was what they'd dubbed him. Poor Dog seemed to be part German shepherd, part something else, with sharp ears and nose, more black than brown. He lay outside almost every evening, on a short leash, following the movements of passers-by with his eyes. Otto fantasized about releasing him and taking him along, bringing him home. Supplying him with food and love, walks in the park together, giving Poor Dog a good home. A dog that would lay his head on his feet. But Poor Dog already had an owner. A beefy guy with tattoos on his arms and further up under his neck where the blue and red images met at bulging arteries. So Otto steered clear, always steered clear. I've never rescued anyone, he thought.

'A cosy little bistro,' Sofie repeated disdainfully. 'You know, yesterday when I was coming through the gate, there was a man pissing inside. In broad daylight. He just stood there, rocking on his heels and pissing right where I was about to come in. Do you think anyone is going to open up a cosy bistro in a place like this?'

'What did you do? Did you yell at him?'

'Yell at a man with his dick out?'

'No, you couldn't have done that. You probably just waited patiently for him to finish.'

'No, I didn't! I took a long bike ride, I rode around Kampen, I was so angry. I didn't come back until the piss had soaked into the ground, but the stench was still there. It's there now!'

They were on their way in through the wrought-iron gate. The gate screeched on its hinges. It did smell like piss.

'In that case, maybe we should move up there,' said Otto. 'To Kampen. Maybe we should actually, seriously consider it?'

Sofie didn't respond as they pushed the bikes to the stand. Behind them, the birch trees rustled. The two birches were the pride of the inner court-yard. Some yellow leaves had fallen onto the large garden table, wasn't it still too early? But the late summer had been dry.

'We're not exactly getting any younger,' Otto continued. 'In a few years, these stairs may be too much for us.'

He could tell by the way she rattled the bicycle lock that she didn't like what he said. When Sofie spoke about herself and her husband with others, she tended to say she was in her mid-forties and he in his mid-fifties, although the truth was that she was nearing fifty and he would soon be sixty. Otto thought she was actually in denial, refusing to believe that they were getting older. He had once ventured an earnest discussion on the topic. But Otto, we will be old for such a long time, she had said. We will be old for so long, maybe even for

24

decades, isn't that a long enough time to be old? Must we have to start *before* it's time? He didn't have anything to say to that, he couldn't say what he'd been thinking. That they *were* already old. That they'd been flung into premature old age when they'd lost Marie.

After ascending the stairs, Sofie headed into the kitchen to put on water for tea. Otto slumped down in the reading chair and was soon deep into his papers. He didn't even notice when Sofie set a cup down on the table opposite him. Not until the tea had turned cold and she had already turned in.

NIGHT

Sofie didn't know at first what woke her. The room was dark and the street outside was silent. She couldn't recall what she'd been dreaming. Next to her, Otto's breath was steady and calm. Sofie tried to stop thinking. If she could manage to disconnect her thoughts and relax, she may be able to fall asleep again. She turned over onto her side and relaxed her body. That's when she noticed the pounding in her arm. Well, perhaps it wasn't exactly pounding, but there was something, a pressure. She could feel her heartbeat in her chest and right arm. That was the arm with the bite. She touched it with her left hand. The right arm was warm, and maybe a bit swollen just above her wrist. That must have been the reason she awoke. She had been lying on her arm and it had fallen asleep. She exhaled calmly and tried to drift off again. To glide away from the bed, from her thoughts, from everything that kept her there.

But there isn't any prickling, thought Sofie. There's usually a prickling sensation when the nerves have been pinched and reawaken. She rose and padded to the bathroom. She switched on the light, sat on the toilet seat and heard more than felt a thin stream tinkling down. She should probably give up drinking tea in the evenings. Even the mild green teas could make the body uneasy. She held her arms out in front of her, compared them without noticing much difference. There was some swelling around the bite itself, more like a kind of bulge or lump. No red ring, no hint of the bite itself. That's when it became dangerous, if there was a red ring around it. She couldn't go to the doctor with this. A small lump that she had scratched until it bled. Sofie dried herself, walked to the sink and leant her forehead towards the mirror, allowing cool water to run down her wrist and hands. She found some antiseptic in the cupboard, the bottle was almost empty. It had been there for ages. And now it was diluted, too old, probably wouldn't have any effect. She poured what was left in the bottle directly onto the wound. Most of it ran off and down into the sink. She would have to remember to buy more. And iodine too. Wasn't iodine even stronger? She shuffled down to the kitchen and found the note block with the shopping list on the shelf above the stove, began to write a list. Pyrisept. Iodine. It looked alarming, so she hurried to jot down a few other items. Detergent. Olive oil.

The kitchen, like everything else, seemed altered at night. The harsh light above the counter didn't reach far, at least not into the living room. Otto's jacket, which he had hung across the chair, seemed like a presence. It was as if the chair and the jacket had merged to form a new constellation, a kind of half-animated creature watching her, following where she went from window to window, peering out. What was it that she hoped would materialize outside? Something unusual. That was what she wanted. A surprise. Change. Her eyes had tired of these rows of houses, these rooftops of varying heights and construction cranes rendering the horizon. These lifeless, slumbering streets. She wanted to grab hold and pull it aside, like a stage curtain, peek at what was behind. A new city. New night skies. Or a wide, open plain with rippling grass. One becomes what one sees. She felt herself petrified like the darkened city.

But she could sense that the darkness was about to retreat. *That*, at least, was a change. The darkness retreated, just as it always did when it was time. Yet the darkness was never very far away, it simply recoiled, ducked down behind the mountain ridges, inside the entryway, only to unfurl again and blanket everything. Now it gathered near the horizon, thickened there, prepared for its retreat. Sofie leant her forehead against the glass, realized that they had just washed the windows. It would leave a mark. She yawned, leant harder against the glass, could feel the turmoil stirring inside her, tried to put a name on it. Mild anxiety, perhaps. If there was such a thing as mild anxiety, then it must be related to light melancholy. Who was it who had talked about light melancholy? And what was that supposed to mean? Sofie breathed deeply, in and out. Another mark on the glass, the steam from her breath. She kissed the mark, and there was a mark inside the mark, from her lips. A light melancholy must be that type of fatigue and sorrow that came over one at night, preferably a bright, warm summer night after the guests have gone and the glasses have been cleared away, the tablecloth removed from the table. When one becomes aware, all at once, that the evening has been a success but also, now, that it is over.

A white delivery truck drove slowly up the street. The sight of this kind of vehicle could still trigger panic in her. But soon she heard the sound of the daily newspaper bundles being pitched out at the plaza with the dried-up fountain. That's where the blue newspaper carts were stored, leant up against a fence. Soon they would be squeaking out towards the entire neighbourhood. It was so fragile, the dim morning light, that thin membrane covering everything just before it burst. In the first years, these nightly ventures had had a different rhythm, shorter. She had been haunted by intolerable thoughts and an aching back, she'd had to pace rapidly back and forth if only at least to clear a path. Now her blood and thoughts flowed more calmly, more freely. She could look at their block of flats like a ship carrying a load of sleeping passengers on board, on its way through unknown waters, on its way through darkness towards a new day, a new harbour. But suddenly it was no longer a ship sailing through the night, it was life itself, full steam ahead.

It's true that sorrow decreases with time. It's also true that sorrow grows larger.

Sofie paced back and forth between the living room and office. The rooms seemed so empty, despite the colourful pictures adorning the walls, the stylish furniture, the quirky little statues and busts she'd inherited from her grandfather and arranged on shelves and pedestals. On the table, a bouquet of marigolds screaming their orangeness. In the windowsill, a vase of snapdragons, pastel and delicate as glass. Still, the room lacked life. Traces of people, quite simply. Toys on the floor, crumbs pressed into the carpeting, backpacks and discarded bags, packages of butter that had been out for too long on the countertop, sports equipment blocking the way in the hall, furniture standing askew because of the whirlwind which was constantly spinning through the room. It lacked life because there was no one there. Only ghosts, shadows. Only all that could have been.

Only the two of them. Otto and she. And that question she always tried to escape. She had become good at thinking without thinking, she had practised it now for years. But sometimes the question pressed itself upwards, and in the creeping morning light, it snuck up on her again. Should they have stayed in the house where Marie had lived together with them? When they made their decision, it had been absolutely clear to Sofie that she couldn't continue living in a place that contained so many memories. And so, it meant that she had to move away from the house where her daughter had hopped, slept, played, snacked, cried, sung. Sofie leant against the bookcase, knocked her head lightly against the books. She would still insist now that it was a decision she'd simply had to take. Which didn't mean it wasn't painful. It didn't mean that the wound wasn't reopened every single day. Just recently, filling out a form, she had come across a question about whether she had children. She had stood there, unmoving and staring at the form, unable to complete it. One of two boxes to cross out, yes or no. She didn't know whom she should ask. And what would she have asked, in any case? Tell me, do I have children? Or do I not?

She had given away almost everything, only a few small boxes had been allowed to accompany them when they moved. They had moved away from the sticker marks where Marie had secretly stuck her stickers on the wall near her bed, the chip in the floor she had made that time she was trying on her new figure skates in the house, the broad window seat where they liked to sit together and drink hot chocolate on rainy days.

And there were more questions. Once, they had gained entry into her thoughts . . . Should she have been more determined to have another child? Yes, she should have. Of course they should have had another child, she and Otto, a child together before it was too late. But first he had refused, with

31

surprising vehemence, and later it had been she who'd hesitated. They had never been synchronized on that matter. Sofie hugged her arms again, the area around the bite was warm. Inflammation. Something her body had to deal with, sleeping or awake. Otto would only worry unnecessarily if he knew that it had been a tick bite. He would have made a fuss. The tick had been quite small, she had tried to pluck it out, but there was most likely a small bit of the creature still lodged inside. Everything would turn out well once she got around to washing it thoroughly.

She would leave the newspaper lying on the doormat, try to get a few more hours of sleep, to greet the morning together with Otto. Sofie crept quietly back up the stairs and to the bathroom, found the peg for her robe. There was enough pale light through the blinds for her to see a dark figure in the mirror, a girl in a short, blue dress. The dress was actually a long T-shirt, washed and worn to a threadbare, soft cocoon. Soon she would have to throw away her favourite nightgown and she would never find anything to replace it.

The bed was cold. She had been away for too long.

FRIDAY

Otto did not wake her with a cup of coffee as he almost always did. When she came downstairs to the kitchen, he was sitting, spectacles pushed far down atop his nose, staring at his mobile phone.

'What's going on?'

'I'm trying to get a hold of Peter. He sent me a text message and asked me to call him as soon as possible. But he won't pick up.'

Sofie considered.

'Nine hours . . . Which means it's afternoon, evening over there. Did he write anything else?'

Though Otto was tapping on the keys in his customary slow and thoughtful manner, the furrow on his brow was deeper than usual, and his lower lip was thrust forward. He didn't respond, so Sofie began to bring the shiny coffee machine to life. It soon began gurgling and hissing, a routine morning melody which she usually heard from the bedroom upstairs That bubbling sound, and thereafter the aroma of coffee and Otto's footsteps up the stairs. His daily morning gift to her. But now his tension hung like a thin fog in the kitchen. Father and son usually maintained a fixed ritual. Otto would call every other Sunday, and on rare occasions Peter might send a text message. Sofie stirred a teaspoon of sugar into each cup, she had taken out the large, white cups with patterns on the inside, a rose in one, a summer bird in the other. She liked to fill the cups, watch the tiny symbols vanish and then reappear as she sipped. As she placed one of the cups before Otto, she noticed that his hair, which had recently become markedly thinner, was tousled and web-like. He sent his message and sat staring vacantly into the room. She sat down on the other side of the table and captured his gaze.

'It could be anything.'

Otto sighed. 'Yes, it definitely could be anything.'

'In any case, it's certainly not what you're most afraid of.'

'Which is?'

'If something had gone wrong with the dive, someone else would have contacted you.'

Otto sighed again. 'And it can't be about money either. Because in that case it wouldn't be so urgent.'

Sofie knew that this was a sore topic. Peter rarely repaid money that he borrowed from his father, something which had always been a deep source of irritation for Otto. Not because Otto couldn't live without the money, but because it made it so evident that his son, at the age of thirty, still hadn't taken control of his own life. When Peter had moved to Australia to study, Otto had initially been happy to contribute towards the high tuition fees. But his son never took his exams, he switched majors several times, and as the years passed so did the suspicion that his time was more often spent surfing and partying. When Otto made it clear that he would no longer finance such a lifestyle, Peter dropped his studies altogether and began working as a diving instructor.

'Maybe he decided it was time to come home for a visit. It's been a while since the last time.'

'Christmas two years ago.'

'Mm-hmm. That Christmas.'

Otto lay down his mobile phone and grasped the coffee cup.

'I've sent a text and left a message on his answering machine. There's not much more I can do right now.'

'Maybe you could call Emma. He would probably contact his mum if there was something serious?'

Otto sat unmoving, but Sofie could see that he was rearing up internally. Suddenly he leant across the table and grabbed for her hands. She was barely able to set down her coffee cup before he found and squeezed both of her small hands between his own.

'Sofie, I don't want to talk with anyone but you. You know that. I would give so much to talk with no one else but you. No one but you in the whole world.'

Sofie was about to say something, but Otto released her hands just as quickly as he'd taken them, and walked out of the kitchen. She heard the door to the tiny hallway toilet, the key turning. It was his place. The only sign that Otto was also a tormented soul was his bad digestion. Sofie finished her coffee and spread jam on a piece of bread, which she ate standing up. This could turn into a fine day. The sky was shifting, the layer of clouds was starting to break. A thin strip of sunlight rested above Nesodden like a gleaming spike. Sofie put away the food and hurried to the washroom to put on her make-up. Returning to the downstairs hall, she could still hear the silence inside the small toilet.

'It's too bad we couldn't go to the cabin today! The weather looks as though it may be nice, despite the forecast.'

She spoke aloud as she tried on a few of the jackets that hung there. The old dress jacket she'd bought in a vintage boutique might work. The arms were so long that they covered her wrists. Even when she stretched out her arms.

'I'm sure it'll be lovely at Ingvild and Gunnar's,' said a voice from inside.

'Of course. Promise to call me as soon as you hear from Peter!'

'I promise.'

Sofie wanted to add that he should remember to run a comb through his hair before going to work but she refrained. That would offend him, and he would forget in any case.

She sprinted lightly down the stairs. The block of flats had been completely renovated, but the developer had fortunately had the sense to keep the high, narrow windows lining the stairwell. There was a special glazing on the old glass. The rippled surface made the birches behind them appear greener than they really were, they were encompassed by a glow.

She longed to be out in the green countryside, out in the wide open spaces. There were too many bushes and thickets around their cabin, according to Otto, and after having discovered more ticks than usual on her person during the summer, Sofie agreed that they needed to tidy things up. But not too much, she liked that the cabin was so concealed. Now she longed to get in her car and drive down, to pull a deck chair over beneath the crooked pine, nap or read a book, make coffee the old-fashioned way. Why did they go and attend all of these dinner parties? They couldn't use the cabin on those weekends when they had a Saturday engagement, even though the drive was only a little over an hour.

Sofie heard the heavy outer door click into the lock behind her. It was still humid, there was an indefinable weight in the air. She halted in the courtyard to enjoy the sight of the birches. That light rustle among the birch trunks. And the narrow treetops filtering light from thousands of tender leaves. She inhaled deeply. Only one more working day, then it would be the weekend.

Up on the fifth floor, Otto could tell that Sofie was leaving. First the sound of footsteps gone on the stairs, and then this dull pain which her physical separation from him always inflicted. As though each parting held the risk of never seeing her again. The pain or the twinge or whatever he might call it, this sense that it was a part of himself that was walking out the door, had never diminished with the years. Never did he harbour stronger emotions for her than when she said goodbye and disappeared, and this thing which they had together stretched further and further. Whenever he lost sight of her, or the sound of her vanished, he would feel that sense of panic: Now, right in this moment, now he'd lost her.

He looked around, the small WC was wall-papered with their life. The green-painted walls were covered with pictures, hung haphazardly, some with and others without frames. Those without had yellowed, edges warped and fraying, there were photos and clippings from magazines and newspapers. He had been sitting there studying a mini interview of himself in one of the daily papers when he had received news about his new position as leader at FROM, the Foundation for the Romani. That was five years ago, but he looked much younger in the photo than he felt nowadays. Otto shook his head at the interview. Favourite tune: 'Power to the People'. Last read book: *Moby-Dick*. They had the book at home, but had he really read it in its entirety? He had most likely come up with the title because his eyes had rested on the thick spine of the book on the shelf. What would he answer if they were to ask him today? The last thing he had read was a book about genocide.

His legs protested as he stood. Otto was stiff from sitting for so long. He checked his mobile phone in the kitchen. No messages. He found Emma's number, she picked up immediately. That familiar, sharp voice. He dropped the usual salutations and asked outright if she'd heard from Peter.

'No . . . Is something wrong?'

'He just asked me to call him but isn't picking up.'

'But that's not unusual, is it?'

A slight tremor in her voice. Shit, now he had her frightened too.

'He just sent one of his rare messages, and it came during the night. But it's probably nothing. He's probably just at work.'

Otto waited. Emma remained silent in *that* way.

'I'm just wondering . . . ' she began. 'The last time we spoke, he said something about going to get checked out at the doctor's'

Otto leant against the window-sill, which cut into his thigh and sent a pang through his body, a prick of here and now.

'But he said that it was only a routine check-up,' Emma continued.

It was quiet for a while.

'Otto?'

'Yes, I'm here.'

'I'll try to call him.'

'No, Emma, I can call him. I'm the one he tried to get a hold of. There's no point in making a big deal out of this. It could be about money, for all I know. I'll just call you once I've spoken with him.'

Otto lay down his phone and rubbed his hands together. They were clammy and cold. Outside, the sun shone on the cluttered rooftops. Two gulls fought over something on the roof of the building where the pub was located, cater-cornered across the street. After a brief scuffle, one of them flew off, a long morsel dangling from its beak. The other remained, poking its head forward and letting out long, aggrieved shrieks. In the unfinished building next door, the crane swung soundlessly from side to side, with enormous concrete blocks sagging from its lengthy maw. Otto looked at the clock. It was only half an hour until the inspection. He would have to drop breakfast and take a taxi, there was nothing else he could do.

The clock on his mobile phone showed 9.43. They were met with a crest of red lights, the taxi sat hemmed in on Kirkeveien. He should have taken the subway, it would have been just as quick. Half the street was invariably closed off, they were always drilling and razing in this city, although the

residents weren't left with the impression that anything was changing for the better.

Otto caught a glimpse of himself in the
rearview mirror and could see some tufts of hair
sticking up in back. He tried discreetly to smooth
the hair. Peter had been lucky, he had inherited
his mother's hair, thick, dark curls. Brown eyes.
Strong chin. Not much of the father there. He had
turned into a stranger, and Otto never should have
accepted the way things had become. But at a certain point in time, it was simply too late for anything. It was the divorce, it had destroyed so much.
His relationship with his son turned into a question
about logistics, regulated by agreements and full
schedules, reduced to pickings-up and droppings-
off and a struggle to fill the short visitation periods
with some kind of activity. Otto wasn't that cre-
ative, unlike Sofie. She would have come up with
things to do, arranged outings, competitions, treasure hunts. She would have shown Peter how to
form shadow puppets and fold origami. Whereas
Otto's imagination had been limited to combing
the video store for movies they could watch
together.

It had been so lovely starting over again with
Sofie and Marie and a nearly adult Peter. A new
chance, days brimming with sun. Those first years
as a single father diminished in his memory, images
of a taciturn little boy who only ever stayed briefly.
The forelock that hung down, always hiding an
eye. But at least he had got the boy out into the

43

fresh air. In the summer, treks into the forest, matches and kindling in their rucksack, sausages for grilling. In the winter, skiing in to Kikut, warm soft rolls while their wet wool stockings and mittens warmed up on the outside oven. Peter never said that he didn't want to come on these trips, or that they were too far for him. But he also never mentioned that he was looking forward to it. He blistered easily. After an especially strenuous ski trip, he had bled right through two pairs of socks. When Emma discovered them she was furious, blamed Otto for abusing the boy. This exhaustive condemnation through which she exposed him. Everything he did was wrong. The wrong films, the wrong shoes. The wrong father, quite simply. Peter never complained. But Otto bought him larger ski shoes, better cross-country skis. The dream of gliding forward, as though wind was pushing at your back. On Sunday after dinner, Peter packed his bag, quiet and serious, without anyone asking him to. Got himself ready. Never forgot anything.

Otto leant back, closed his eyes for a while, could feel everything spinning. Peter, Peter. He had looked so tan and agile when they had visited him last Easter. But at the same time so worn, his face ragged and tense. Too much beer, too much red meat, too much sun and too many arbitrary women, he and Sofie had both remarked. But what did they know? He stared out of the side window.

The streets were like a war zone. Pedestrians and motorists were embattled in getting ahead first. There were so many desperate people out there.

'Tell me, are people more aggressive now than before?'

A glance in the mirror. The driver studied him, wondered what kind of a person he was. Otto had surprised himself with the question, now he regretted asking it.

'Than before what?'

Otto shrugged, mumbled that he thought it had got worse. More pronounced. More apparent. And then the traffic finally broke up. The driver pressed down on the accelerator, broke free in a series of jerky movements, Otto noticed that he was able to inhale all the way down into his stomach. There was no more talk, not until they had exited the arterial street and the driver needed help in locating the tiny side road which led to Mærradalen. At the road's end, a group of people stood around talking, two of them were studying a map.

'Oh,' said the driver leaning forward. 'Is this where the Gypsy camp is? I just read about it in the news.'

'So you have,' said Otto drably. He had given up trying to correct people. No one used the term Romani, he had almost stopped using it himself.

'A bit of a commotion, that is! They're not used to these kinds of things on this side of town.'

'No, you're right about that.'

Could Otto detect a smidgeon of sympathy from the driver? He signed, gave a larger tip than usual.

'Poor devils,' the driver said and handed him the receipt.

Did he mean the Romani people, who would soon have to pack up their belongings once again? Or was his concern more for the people who lived there, and who complained that they were forced to protect their children, their pets and gardens. There had been unrest in this part of the city before, large protests when the city council moved to relocate a couple of Romani families into social housing. As the thermometer crept down to minus twenty degrees that January, they had needed to find temporary housing for someone with small children. It had all turned out well but those people who had warned that it would attract more Romanis to this part of the city would now claim that they had been right.

Several makeshift shelters had been erected since Otto's last visit. Cars and campers were parked helter-skelter down the gully, and the area around the community campfires stirred with activity. He was supposed to determine whether there was anything reprehensible in the way that this encampment had been established. There wasn't much doubt as to the outcome of the discussion. Of all the complaints that had been issued from neighbours and frequent walkers in the area, the city council put the most emphasis on that of a nearby day-care, which could no longer take excursions through the small gully.

The council chief waved cordially as he got out of the cab. Otto recognized two people from the Ullern district. The people with the map were from the environmental agency. They were determining whether the camp might be harming the natural diversity in Mærradalen.

Otto finished shaking hands with everyone when his mobile phone rang. He reached into his pocket with one hand and waved the rest of the group onward with the other.

'It's you, finally. Is there something going on?'

'Yes, it's not *that* urgent.'

Peter's voice was artificially pleasant. Ah, so it was about money. Otto felt relieved and disappointed at the same time. He walked slowly downward, maintaining a good distance from the others who were nearly down to the encampment.

'No, I need a bit of help. . . with some health insurance . . . '

'Health insurance? Is something ailing you? Your mother said you've been to the doctor!'

'So you've talked to Mama?'

Mama. It always sounded so strange when grown men said mama.

'I just called to hear if you'd been in touch with her. Your message came in the middle of the night,

47

and I was worried when I couldn't get a hold of you.'

'And then she said there was something wrong with me?'

'No, she just said that you had to go to the doctor. For a routine check-up.'

'That's right. A routine check-up.'

Otto wondered whether he should delve deeper. It was always like this. So much that he wished to say, and so little that he was able to say, and he would soon have to hang up. Help me, Peter, he thought. Say something. But there was nothing but an atmospheric pressure against his ears.

'Peter?'

'Sorry, the connection is a bit bad. The problem is that I don't have real insurance, it's not like it is in Norway.'

'Have you really never got that all straightened out . . . '

He stopped himself. What difference did it make to scold? Peter said something, but his voice faded into static. Otto turned and tried walking back up the hill again.

'Peter, I can't hear you very well. Is there any-thing particular that you have to have checked? Could you please explain it a bit better?'

' . . . physical examination,' was all that Otto heard.

'Peter, Peter, one more time. A physical examination? Does it have anything to do with work?'

'Yes. I need that kind of thing to renew my licence. A full exam. And it's pretty expensive.'

His voice was clear again now. Otto stood midway up the hill and felt more helpless than he had for a long time. If Peter hadn't figured out his health insurance, what had he figured out?

'It's all fine, Papa. I'm in good shape.'

Papa. This tiny word went in for attack. His throat constricted. Otto swallowed.

'Well, Peter, of course I'll help you. Send me a message about how much you need, and I'll transfer it into your account as soon as I'm home.'

'Thank you. Thank you so much. And I would appreciate it if you wouldn't mention this to Mama.'

'Why not? I can't promise you that. She's going to ask me, and I don't want to lie to her. You can understand that?'

Nothing but static. But he was still there.

'Take care, Peter. I'm thinking of you.'

His phone slipped into his pocket like a sleek fish. A couple of kids were on their way over to him, one of them was a girl of seven or eight years whom he had entertained a bit last time, he had got her to laugh. Now she came leading her younger brother. Both wore striped vests patched with grass stains. They radiated gravity. There were not many children in the camp, they didn't have many other playmates. The small boy toddled towards him determinedly with a few blades of grass protruding from between his clenched fist.

Children. Knowing them, protecting them. That's what it's all about. Otto squatted down.

'Hi there,' he said, and smiled.

Sofie met Otto in the doorway. She hugged him, said nothing, just held around his waist and embraced him strongly. He had to drop his bag to put his arms around her too. She was barefoot and had changed into the dark-grey dress that was a kind of terry cloth, soft to the touch. It was Friday evening. They were going to stay in. It was time for drinks.

'What will it be today?' he asked into her hair.

She extracted herself from his arms and looked up playfully.

'Rum and cola.'

'Rum and *cola*?'

'I had one at a bar the other day, and it was actually good.'

'Really, Sofie. I expected something more sophisticated from you.'

She vanished into the living room. 'Wait and see!' she called over her shoulder.

Otto followed, as he liberated himself from everything that was heavy and restrictive. His dress jacket landed on the back of a chair, his necktie around a bust that Sofie's grandfather had made. The beautiful profile and unnaturally long neck had been modelled after a film star who no one could remember the name of any longer, but she

51

looked good in his tie. Out in the kitchen, chips of ice tinkled. It had become a competition of sorts. Each Friday, when there weren't other plans, they took turns mixing drinks. Sofie was good at finding new recipes, and was happy to scour the city for ingredients. Otto's method was to develop and perfect the drinks that he was already able to make. His goal was to create Oslo's best dry martini. He had discussed various methods with several bartenders around the city, and scoffed at anyone who tossed the vermouth directly into the glass. He himself tossed the vermouth out into the sink after trickling it over the ice chips. Rum and cola. How could she sink so low?

Sofie merely laughed. She walked into the living room with two tall glasses. Green wedges of lime bobbed in the black liquid. She hadn't even taken the trouble to squeeze the lime peel against the glass, as he had shown her to do. The point was that only the oil from the peel was supposed to be added. Otto raised the glass sceptically to his nose.

'Just as I thought. It smells by and large like drunken youth.'

'Don't smell, taste. This is not cheap rum, it's the real thing.'

He sipped. In spite of the lime it was mostly sweet. Sofie took a solid swig.

'Ah, the weekend at last.'

'Yes, the memories are flooding back. Weekends, and long road trips to parties miles and miles away. Crammed in the backseat with an illegal number of passengers and a bottle of booze passed around. The smell of moonshine and jeans that hadn't been washed in weeks. And on the way home, the aroma of puke.'

'Cheers, country boy.'

'Cheers, city girl.'

Their ritual exchange of familiar phrases. Why did it give Sofie a vague feeling of irritation only today? She dismissed the annoyance. Weren't these phrases part of the glue that held them together? That's the way we are, they said. This is us.

She studied Otto over the rim of her glass. He looked exhausted. Grey. His voice on the phone had sounded listless when he'd called her at work that afternoon.

'Were you able to talk to Peter at all?'

'No, but Emma was. I asked her not to call him until I knew if it was something serious. But she threw herself onto the telephone and turned everything into a little drama. So much fuss about such a small trifle.'

'If it is a trifle.'

'What do you mean by that?'

'No, I don't know. You're the one who spoke with him.'

Otto frowned. 'He said it was just a routine check-up.'

'And he needs health insurance for that?'

'That has to do with his job. I think it's that the people who work as instructors are required to undergo thorough examinations. After all, the conditions of their job expose them to a great deal of stress.'

'That is true.'

Otto sunk into the sofa, unbuttoned another button on his shirt. Sofie sat in the chair opposite, fixing her gaze on him. She had never really figured out what Otto meant by saying that he had such a bad relationship with his son. He had related some stories, things that were completely normal, about how he had taken the boy on ski trips that were much too long and hadn't been good at helping him with homework. Sins no worse than those of which other parents were guilty. Sofie tried getting him to talk more about it, but he would only say that he didn't understand it all himself. When they moved in together, Otto had been very clear about not having any more children. She had chosen not to press him. As she expected, he adjusted his position after a while. Sofie was certain it was because he had established such a good relationship with Marie.

'Have you thought about what we should do for dinner today?' he asked, visibly uncomfortable beneath her gaze.

'Maybe we could order from the new Peruvian place?'

'That's too far away for pick-up. And we had fish yesterday . . . '

'So that means that you'd like Thai?'

'Yes, maybe Thai?'

'If you want Thai, then just order Thai. You don't have to hold an election if you already know what you want.'

He looked at her, offended. 'If you have such a strong opinion about it, then . . . '

'I don't. Just go for it and order.'

'Well, someone obviously needs to get food into their system!'

Otto struggled up off the sofa and walked into the hallway to get his mobile phone. The sound of ice rattling in an empty glass indicated that Sofie was on her way into the kitchen to mix herself a new drink. She knew it as well as he did— every Friday would always be a black Friday, no matter how much they tried to jazz it up. Their mixed-drink competition was merely an excuse to hasten the intoxication, in order to gain respite, to forget. It usually ended with Sofie extinguished on the sofa and Otto sitting alone with his shot glass in hand, watching TV. He put in the order, unsure whether the person who had picked up had actually taken note of what he wanted. On his way through the library, he stopped next to Sofie's small desk. A cream-coloured envelope protruded from a stack of paper. French stamps, Otto pulled it out. Leon always wrote by hand, always with a fountain pen.

It looked like a thick letter. Otto shoved it back between the other papers. Strange that Sofie hadn't mentioned it.

She had slid back in the chair. Her eyes closed. Her hands resting in her lap, and Otto registered a yellow fleck on her wrist. Iodine? That didn't look very good at all.

'It seems there are more people than just me who've had a heavy day,' he ventured.

Sofie replied without opening her eyes. 'It was completely fine. There weren't many ministers or journalists at the official opening today, but that didn't exactly come as a surprise.'

'But you got to give your opinion about it.'

She squinted out through dark, heavy eyelashes. 'I didn't say a word, are you insane? That wouldn't come across very well. No, no. I bought marzipan cake and brewed the coffee, like the good manager that I am.'

'But, did you speak with Karin?'

Sofie sat up. 'I always speak with Karin.'

'I mean, properly? About the friction between the two of you?'

'I wouldn't exactly call it friction.'

'But Karin does.'

'What did you say?'

'Karin calls it friction.'

Sofie's eyes widened. 'Have *you* spoken to Karin?'

'Yes, I spoke with her a bit yesterday. During the concert.'

Sofie pushed her glass to the side and leant forward across the table. She moved her lips, couldn't find any words.

'Come on, Sofie, it's Karin. Of course I speak with her! She used to pop in and out of here, she's even accompanied us to our cabin. For two days, and in that amount of time she managed to deck every single surface with her scarves and make-up and shoes.'

'You . . . So you've spoken to Karin. About me. And you did that yesterday? You didn't tell me yesterday.'

Sofie's voice had lost all intonation. Otto regretted not having waited until after dinner to bring all of this up.

'I'm telling you now. Is that so terrible?'

'We talked about this yesterday on our way home. But you didn't say anything about that conversation then. And that makes me think it must have been an extra special conversation, since you let a day pass before mentioning it to me.'

'Take it easy, it was very brief. Karin asked me how you were doing lately. If you were well, I can't remember how exactly she formulated it. But it seemed to me as though she was fishing around a bit, in order to find out whether it had anything to do with her. Whether you were angry at her or something, or if it was just that you weren't doing so well. That's how I understood it.'

As he spoke, fumbling somewhat because he realized that it was extremely important how he chose his words, Sofie stood up and began to pace around the room. She walked in a hunch, as though her stomach were in pain.

'But, please, Sofie dear, it was reasonable for her to try to understand what's going on!'

Sofie stopped and pointed a finger at him.

'Understand what's going on? I'm having a work conflict with one of my employees, with whom I also had a friendship. She feels like she was passed over, which is completely understandable. But she has chosen to deal with it by going around in secret, creating alliances with people who have been supportive of me, luring me into situations that put me into a bad light, and making my work more difficult for me. And then she goes around acting as though she's worried about how I'm doing! Has she recruited you for her team, now? Don't you see how damn duplicitous that is?'

Otto rubbed his chin, hard. He let his hands fall into his lap, where they stayed like an empty, open shell.

'Sofie, I'm not playing on any team, you know that. And I'm not conspiring with your friends or enemies. Karin asked me something, and I responded in a rounded, diplomatic manner, as I usually do. There's absolutely no reason to point your finger at me!'

'But, if it was such a blameless conversation, why didn't you mention it at all yesterday? Don't you see that I find it strange, when we were walking after the opening and discussing what had happened, and we even talked about Karin, that you didn't say a peep about how she went around trying to tap you for information?'

'To tap me . . . I took it to be a sincere question, and I don't believe that I said anything wrong. But it may be that, somewhere inside of me, I knew that you were going to fly off the wall when you learnt that the conversation had taken place.'

'And what does that say about me, exactly?'

'What it says about you? Now I really don't understand . . . '

'What does it say about me, that you don't dare to discuss a conversation that you are very aware would interest me to know about?'

'Sofie, we're discussing it now. You're making it into . . . '

Sofie threw her arms into the air. 'Don't you understand that the absolute worst thing is to be excluded? I'm in a vulnerable position. You can't just go behind my back like that.'

'Ex-cuse me.' Otto's voice was cold. 'But however you choose to interpret this, perhaps you should know that it wasn't my intention to oppose you.'

He moved to get up, but she was quicker.

'I'll pick up the food. I need some air.'

The Thai take-away restaurant was only two blocks away, not far enough for Sofie to calm down. Her hands trembled as she removed her wallet from her purse. The same married couple was always there, working in the steam and the smoke behind a partition. The woman came forward smiling, carrying a thin plastic bag. There were only two boxes in it, and Sofie had a feeling of seeping hopelessness. Hadn't he ordered more food? Two portions wasn't much, he should know that. She asked whether it would be possible to get a starter as well, something that didn't take long to prepare? Yes, she could have some spring rolls. Sofie ordered a double portion and sat down at the locale's sole table.

A ragged weekly magazine was on the table, along with one of the daily papers, a kissing photo across the front spread. A real hit, no doubt about that. She hadn't been able to bring herself to tell Otto about the peculiar mood at the museum that day, in which everyone in the department had gaped at her in such an odd, expectant manner. The strained atmosphere could also be attributed to the presence of the director, who had come to celebrate with them. But why did they look at Sofie as if she were always coming to ruin the party and the jovial mood? They should know that she was the one who had ordered the enormous marzipan cake that they were about to delve into. And as she stood there searching for the right words to use in commenting on both exhibition openings, not least the one that some, evidenced by the front page spread that she now held in her hands, described as legendary, she recalled something that Karin had said. You have been nicknamed 'The Nun', she had said, with a disarming laugh, and Sofie had smiled. It was only natural that an entire world of opinions about her would exist, the way that she spoke, her black dresses, her perfume, her manner of walking, opinions that she had no way of influencing, which she wouldn't even have been able to guess at. But now she could read an expression in their eyes which frightened her, a lack of expectation. As if they all knew what she was about to say. As if nothing that she might say or do could alter their perception of her. She could have danced a little jig without anyone so much as lifting an eyebrow. It was a desperate feeling, that everything stood fixed.

She hadn't danced a jig for them. But she had delivered a short speech in which she pointed out a connection between the kiss, which they had all witnessed the previous evening, and the kiss as a motif in Munch's work. She spoke about the picture where a couple is kissing, twisted tightly in a large window. The dark blue secretiveness of the kiss and the pure, mild light out on the street. It was one of the few paintings by Munch in which the closeness between a man and a woman seemed harmonious and good. There was usually always this blurred boundary between the erotic and fate,

61

love and cannibalism. *Kiss* stood in stark contrast to, for example, *The Kiss of Death* and *Vampire*. And here, Sofie was on the home stretch. She spoke until she was warm, and felt that she had been able to speak warmth into the staff. The director had followed up with praise and grand visions. But Sofie still had a limp, aching feeling in her heart, almost as if she had been exercising.

She turned the newspaper over. The weather forecast on the back was full of angry, dark clouds. There had been talk throughout the week of an early autumnal storm expected to come over the southern part of the country, bringing an exceptional amount of precipitation. It had been so dry in the last months, so there were many who would welcome the rain. But these storms were unpredictable. Sofie was uneasy about what was coming. The rain had begun to sprinkle down on the pavement outside. It hissed behind the partition. Sofie sat utterly famished and weak. Two drinks on an empty stomach had shot up her blood sugar levels, but after the fight with Otto, she was only nauseous and dizzy. She could still feel the eyes boring into her skin, the eyes of her colleagues, of Karin, of Otto. That enormous compulsion that people have to know someone in and out, to be the one who understands, who's in the know.

A squeak of styrofoam, and the spring rolls were ready to go. Outside, the rain fell in a drizzle but the sky was bulking up, a grey clenched fist above the rooftops. This will make the Farmer happy, thought Sofie. That's something her father always said when it began to rain. He, the publishing editor, who had never once set foot in a field. And he didn't spend much time out in his garden either, seldom ventured further than the terrace with his books and newspaper. After her mother got arthritis, it fell to Sofie and her sister to take turns tending the large garden in the Bestum neighbourhood. During dry spells, like this one that had lasted well over a month, they had to water almost every other day. She was responsible this week. She'd been putting it off for a bit too long, and a few days ago she had received an angry message from her sister. Because Sofie had never turned up, their father had gone loose on the garden with the hose. He had watered too much, and many of the flowers, the most delicate ones, had toppled over for good. The loss extended in particular to the fine bed of peas, the message informed her. Sofie knew that Judit had spent time helping their mother tie them up. She hadn't responded to the message yet.

A warm wind swept through the buildings, rustled her dress, lifted up a large cardboard box that lay in the street. The rain began to surge. The advanced guard had taken the city. She no longer needed to think about the garden. The rain was getting the job done.

Otto had set the table. Sofie had taught him how. Coordinating colours, symmetry. The wine bottle had fogged up, it was so cold. Sofie dropped the food on the counter.

'Is this right, though?' Otto said, ruffling the bag.

'I'm starving, so I had to order extra,' Sofie yelled on her way to wash her hands.

They munched on the spring rolls as they listened to the growing intensity of the rain outside. They heard it, they saw it, they smelt it. It smelt almost like smoke. A grey tapestry of rain. A song began circling in Otto's head, he thought it must be something about rain, but he couldn't remember the words. He hummed quietly, the melody was there, but the words? Sofie cocked her head.

'Oh, that! That's such a nice one.'

Together they hummed the refrain.

'And I think it's going to rain today,' Sofie fumbled at the ending.

'Yes, that's how it went.' Otto remembered the previous verse too. 'Wasn't it something like: Human kindness is overflowing . . . '

And they sang in chorus: ' . . . And I think it's gonna rain today.'

Otto saw the corners on Sofie's mouth start to turn down. He hurried to remove the top from the red and green curry. She blinked quickly and helped herself.

'Strange, I'd almost forgotten that song.'

They ate for a while without speaking. Rain was always difficult. Sweet memories were hard to separate from bitter ones. The first dance they danced together outside, in the rain. The walks they had taken through the forest, in the rain. Otto had proposed in the rain, beneath a green umbrella. The first time they had been down to see the cabin, it had rained too. They had liked the rain. The rain could be mild and cleansing. But it had also been raining when Marie had met her fate. That ruthless rain over the island.

'Do you know what I just thought of?' asked Otto. 'I thought of the time that we took Peter and Marie on a walk in the forest. There was one time that it rained and at first Peter didn't want to come along.'

'But didn't that happen more than once?'

'But then he did come, and Marie was extremely flustered, so eager to get to know her new big brother. She held his hand the entire time and chattered nonstop.'

'He was so sweet with her.'

'He thought he was too big to come with us on our outings.'

She remembered it well. The battles that Peter fought with himself, how they manifested themselves in his posture. He was both bothered by and proud of the attention that Marie paid him. The big brother, this new trophy, had only lived with them for a short while. He was sixteen, four years older than Marie, when Sofie first met him. And he was nearing eighteen when Otto and she had decided to move in together. His father had prepared a room for him and said that he could come and go as he wished. Marie loved it that he lived with them. That period should have lasted longer. The golden age.

'There is one small thing that I would like to say,' said Otto. 'And you are going to get angry.'

Sofie set down her chopsticks, lifted the wine glass to her mouth and signalled with her free hand. Have at it!

'I agree with you that I could have mentioned my conversation with Karin earlier yesterday. The reason that I hesitated is that I've been afraid that you may have got into a kind of . . . spiral, a painful spiral, in which you interpret everything that is said and done in the worst possible sense. You have a perspective of the situation of that seems rather fixed, in my opinion. What if it isn't Karin, but some of the others who are creating problems for you? Or maybe that the problem has to do with you, that you don't allow yourself to be open enough?'

'You have a problem believing that the lovely, light-hearted Karin could have a dark side?'

'Try to be serious, Sofie. With regards to Karin, I don't know what to believe. I've even wondered on occasion whether she might be in love with you.'

At first Sofie looked as if she was trying to consider his words, but she wasn't able to, and began to laugh.

'You've completely missed the mark,' she guffawed.

Otto picked up his chopsticks and pointed them at her.

'Think about it.'

'But seriously, where did you come up with *that*? She's had a lot of boyfriends, we've even met several of them.'

'That's just it. Suitors come and go, and to me most of her relationships have seemed like friendships. And she really projects a double signal. But first and foremost, I see that she always wants more from you than you are willing to give. Have you thought about that?'

'No. And I'm not about to, either.'

Sofie continued eating without saying more. Of course she had thought about it. When Otto said that Karin was in love with her, he might have been on to something. But he didn't see the entire picture. The friendship between Sofie and Karin had waned after Sofie applied for and received the position as department manager, but it had already been changing long before that. Sofie came to the Munch Museum following a long period of sick leave. Before that, she had worked at a private gallery. When they moved to the Tøyen neighbourhood, both she and Otto had looked for new jobs. It wasn't enough to move to a completely different side of the city, they wanted to change everything. Karin was the one who had taken care of her, who had helped her back on her feet. For that first period, Sofie was utterly raw. They grew close. Karin was able to endure listening to all of those harsh things, the emotions that Sofie couldn't even tell Otto about. But after a while, Sofie began to have a strange feeling that she was being drained. It wasn't as if she was allowed to empty herself, it was rather that she was being emptied. Karin was too eager, their friendship became too intense. So Sofie had pulled away, slowly and cautiously. It wasn't her that Karin was in love with, it was more something that she *had*. Something that she *was*. Every now and then, Sofie thought perhaps that Karin was in love with her sorrow, but that was one of the things that she couldn't say out loud.

Outside of the half-open windowpane, the rain announced its presence with a monotone sound, and from upstairs they could hear it drumming with impressive force upon the roof. The percussionists of heaven. Otto walked over and shut the window, but continued to look out. Most of the city was hidden behind a veil of grey. His hearing had gone numb. It really was quite a rainstorm.

'This is tropical,' he said. 'Cold, tropical rain, it's unnatural.'

'They say that we had better get used to it.'

'Then in that case I know what we'd best do. We should go out onto the veranda. Bathe in the rain.'

Sofie looked at him, first with a patronizing gaze, but then with more and more disbelief, until her face broke into that expression that he loved, playful, awake. She stood up too, and they sprinted up the stairs. In the bedroom they tore off their clothes and flung them onto the bed. Otto opened the door out to the small, shielded rooftop terrace. The rain was hitting the flagstones so hard that it looked like it was raining both upwards and downwards. He took a first tentative step out onto the terrace. Sofie suddenly thought that he looked old. From the side, she could see that his skin puckered across his stomach, and that he stooped with his back. But once he was outside, he lifted his arms into the air and began dancing around his own axes as he wiggled his white, luminous backside. Sofie shuddered and threw herself out after him. They were soaked through in an instant. It was too late to bring in the pillows on the wicker chairs outside. And the rain was cold. Sofie hopped carefully up and down as she shivered and whimpered.

'Glorious!' Otto teetered over to the high edge. He leant himself outwards, as though wanting to embrace the entire city.

'Watch out, the neighbours can see you now!' shouted Sofie. She gave up hopping and clasped her eyes shut, stood swaying in the rain like an unthinking plant. She stood like this until Otto's arms locked around her. He licked her face and neck and kissed her breasts, which had contracted so it hurt. She didn't open her eyes until he had led her into the bathroom and started rubbing her with a large towel. Her mascara had begun to streak, magnifying her eyes. She looked defenceless. Like a woman who had relinquished everything. He wanted to push her onto the bed, but sensed a resistance in her body that made him uncertain. They had discussed how they shouldn't become one of those married couples who stop having sex. They had managed to keep this pact, even through the heaviest times. But it had become more and more difficult for him to know when he should take the initiative. Sofie rarely opposed his sexual advances but, on the other hand, it was seldom that she approached him in that manner herself. Now he packed both of them into the large bath towel and spoke into her sopping hair.

'Still cold? Would you like to take a shower?'

'No, I would like to crawl under the blanket with you. But I'm afraid that I am just going to sleep.'

'I've been forewarned. I take full and complete responsibility if I'm unable to keep you awake.'

A small sigh, nearly imperceptible. It might be a sigh of surrender, or a sigh of relief, or of despondency, how could he know? How should one interpret these various sighs that people around him delivered? When sighing is just as natural for so many people as breathing? Bound by the towel, they stumbled into the bedroom and plummeted onto the bed.

SATURDAY

The illuminated numbers on the clock radio informed Sofie that she must have been sleeping for at least ten hours. The air thick and humid, the sheets wet with sweat, it had been like lying in a puddle. As if from far off, she pictured the married couple Krohg-Iversen reduced to two dark, water-logged timbers bumping up against each other in an eddy. The rain continued drumming against the skylight. She stretched an arm out across the sheet in search of Otto. Otto was sitting at the edge of the bed, observing her mildly, and gave her arm a light squeeze.

'Come down,' he said. 'They're showing extra broadcasts about the storm tonight. It's bad.'

The television was on down in the living room. Sofie sat on the sofa and pulled a blanket over herself. It took a while until what she viewed on the screen formed any sense of meaning. The image of a large villa taken by the stream and driven downwards along a wild, surging river didn't seem to fit with what the commentator's voice was saying. Otto sat down beside her.

'There may be many casualties,' he said. 'A lot of people are missing.'

'How long have you been up?'

73

'Since around seven. The broadcasts were already going. And now the images have started coming in, as you can see.'

An amateur video showed the river in the process of razing a bridge. The water nearly reached the roadway, upon which a boat, several tree trunks, branches and boards were wedged, jamming up parts of the bridge. The reporter stated that several smaller bridges had been destroyed. A sheriff who was interviewed asked people to stay inside and not to use their cars.

'Where *is* this?'

'Everywhere, almost. The entire eastern part of the country, anywhere where there are rivers. But there has been a lot of damage here in Oslo too. The subway is closed. People have been warned to stay inside until further notice.'

Sofie struggled to stand, and with the blanket wrapped around, walked over to one of the windows. It was no longer raining as heavily as it had the previous night and evening. The city was spread out there, grey and wet beneath the clouds, as on any ordinary rainy day. But the wind still howled and whistled. Behind her, a meteorologist appeared on the screen, explaining how prolonged dry periods could lead to the inability of the earth to absorb the rain. Several experts weighed in. Words that at one time had characterized extremes had now become everyday speech. The experts could just as well have been discussing cheese and crackers.

People appeared to have accepted that these abrupt deluges, frequent storms and weeks of dry spells were now to be taken as the norm.

'First all of these fires,' said Otto. 'And now this.'

Sofie crept back to the sofa again. Soon more updates poured in. The prospects became clearer. Throughout the night, the rivers had swelled at record speed, so quickly that not everyone had time to react. Several residential houses were gone, flushed away, no one knew what had happened to the residents, whether they had managed to escape.

Otto walked into the kitchen to take a few calls. He didn't shut the door, so Sofie could hear that it was about the camp at Ullern. He looked upset when he returned.

'I may have to go out.'

'Don't we have to stay inside?'

'If there is a crisis, then I have to head out. But there's a patrol on its way to check right now.'

'Have you tried to call any of them?'

'Felipe isn't picking up his phone.'

'But the river up there isn't that large, is it?'

'There aren't any small rivers today.'

Otto prepared some toast, which they ate in front of the TV. He chewed without noticing the taste, feeling as though the water was creeping up around his ankles. It was impossible to tear oneself away from the screen, though after a while most of the

reports were mere repetitions. They could stay sitting like this for the entire day, as they had done
during similar televised catastrophes. Otto glanced
over at Sofie. She was blue-white in the light of the
television, a colour like sour milk. She stared at the
screen but seemed to be somewhere else. It's been
eight years, he thought. Eight years and nearly one
month since they sat on the same sofa, but in a different house, on the other side of the city, taking in
another catastrophe on the screen, the start of the
catastrophe that would envelop and take over their
lives. At first it was only smoke, rubble, sirens, dust.
Then a glimpse of people stumbling around, dazed.
Blood on their faces, bloody clothes. The
paramedics and police struggling to take control.
It wasn't long before the first text messages started
buzzing. 'Turn on your TV.' 'Are you all OK?' They
began calling around to family and friends, and
while they assured themselves that those closest to
them were safe, a new tragedy began to unfold, the
one in the rain, on the island.

And they had been worried that she would
catch a cold.

Otto could recount every single second of that
evening, every tiny movement. He had been standing
in the kitchen talking to a friend when he heard a
scream from the living room. The scream turned
into a wail. Otto rushed in and saw that she had
grabbed her phone and was dialling a number. He
realized who she was trying to call when he saw the

text scrolling across the screen, the news about a shooting on an island outside Oslo. She had moved her lips when she heard the voicemail message. And then she hung up and dialled the number again. Over and over. They had sent Marie off the day before. The girl with the much-too-full backpack. She carried the heavy bag as though it was packed with everything that she was in the process of becoming. She bore all of this proudly, out of their sight. She was too young to attend, but had wanted to so much. She was going with two friends who were older. They would sleep in a tent. It was going to be safe. The first day, Sofie and Otto worried constantly, especially because of the heavy rains on Thursday evening. Everything's fine! Marie had laughed into the telephone. Everything's fine, I have boots with me, the concert is starting now, bye!

Sofie called without ceasing. The entire ride out of Oslo. Otto switched channels to find the latest news, trying to find out what was happening, trying to understand. But on the way up towards Sollihøgda, she suddenly began to slam the radio, she hammered the knobs, his arms. He nearly drove off the road. Make it stop, she moaned. Make it stop! He turned off the radio, lay his hand in her lap, she pushed it away. You call, she sobbed. Marie doesn't want to talk to me . . . He had pulled out his mobile phone, put it on speaker phone, called. They listened together to the empty signals, were startled when her voice came. It was as though she was in the car with them. *Hello, you have reached the voice mailbox of Marie Krohg. I cannot come to the phone right now . . .* She sounded so serious, so adult, this silly little girl of theirs. Their quiet ten-year-old. Stubborn and strong. Nothing could possibly happen to her. He called twice more. Sofie cried out loud beside him. He asked if she had the numbers of the girls who had accompanied Marie. Sofie found the number of one of the mothers, her hands trembled. A man picked up. Otto soon realized that the father on the other end was just as frightened as they were. He mostly wanted to end the conversation, because they were also waiting for a call. *That* call. From their girls, who they couldn't reach. But before he hung up, he said that it was important they didn't try calling Marie. The young people out there had requested that no one call them any more.

That's most likely the reason she doesn't pick up, said Otto to Sofie. She's turned it off, she's hiding, maybe she's lost her phone. But his attempt to see it as a good sign only produced more anxiety. That's when they truly understood. They realized the implications, the madness. Realized what was actually happening out there. The kids were fleeing, concealing themselves wherever they could, in hiding, their phones on silent. Ringing might give them away. All around the island, there were rings and beeps on mobile phones. But where there was ringing, he had already been.

They were stopped by the police barricade, they could go no further. 'We're not the ones you should be watching out for!' Sofie screamed in front of a large uniformed policeman. Otto had to get out of the car to restrain her. 'Why aren't you out on the island? Why aren't you taking care of my child?' Sofie had wailed the same sentence over and over again. The policeman was unwavering. Sofie collapsed. She became completely apathetic. They couldn't see the island, but knew that it was out there, behind the police barricade, just behind the bend, just behind the trees, not so far from the mainland. It had been a relief, but it was also uncanny to see the way that other forces took over. For Sofie faded away. Now I'm losing you, Otto had thought. Now I'm losing you too.

The apathy was also present this grey, wet August Saturday, like a spectre lurking in the room. Otto would have liked to turn off the television, but couldn't do it without an explanation. Could he ask her what she was thinking about, how she was doing? She must be thinking the same thing as him.

'It's just as fascinating to see every time. How few seconds it takes nature to annihilate everything,' said Sofie.

He lay a hand on her back. Her narrow backbone, forged of steel. She had remained upright for all of this time. His eyes began to brim. Otto mumbled something and walked out to the tiny hallway toilet. He sat on the seat and waited for the pain to

beckon forth the soothing tears. He heard the telephone ring in the living room, a high-pitched vibra-
tion that always made Sofie jump. She called to him
soon after, apparent irritation in her voice, that his
telephone was ringing. Otto pulled himself together
and blew his nose. Washed his hands and face and
dried off with the small hand towel hanging there.
He noticed too late that the hand towel smelt sour.
The smell stayed in his nose as he walked into the
living room.

'Your phone.'

'Thanks, I could hear both the phone and you
calling.'

Otto took his phone to the kitchen. There was
a message on his voicemail. Someone from the
Labour and Welfare Administration reported that
no one had been hurt, but that there wasn't much
left of the encampment. As Otto listened to the
message, Felipe called. He was quite stirred up, and
it took a while for Otto to understand what he was
saying. From the living room, Sofie could hear how
Otto spoke in his most pedagogical voice, analysing
and minimizing one problem after the other. On the
screen, the water continued sweeping through
buildings and towns, grinding anything it encoun-
tered to smithereens. One story from the centre of
Oslo portrayed volunteers heaping sandbags in the
morning hours around the most exposed buildings
on the lowest parts of the Grünerløkka neighbourhood and in the old part of town. An elderly man

waded around inside his cafe, a helpless attempt to clean up. Akerselva River was unrecognizable, a heaving, mighty deluge unearthing the soil from around large, old tree roots and carving its way menacingly along grey house walls.

'Do you have to venture out?' Sofie asked Otto when he returned and sat down.

'No, the police have been there, and they concluded that there are others who need more help. But I had to call around to my contacts.'

'Are there many children there?'

'No, fortunately not.'

Otto thought about the two that they had met the day before. They must have been frightened. Awake in the middle of the night, hysterical adults, most of their belongings swept away.

'While you were on the phone, two missing people were confirmed dead. And one young boy was found, very exhausted, but alive.'

'Maybe we should turn off the TV for a while?'

Sofie raised her eyebrows. 'And do what? Go for a walk?'

Otto sat on the sofa armrest. There wasn't anything else to do but to stare at the screen, wait for more bad news, hope for small miracles.

'You haven't been to the doctor yet?'

'To the doctor?'

'Yes, to get your bite checked out. It looks like a tick bite to me. Just think of all the ticks we've had on us this summer. Around the cabin, it's crawling with them.'

'Yes, fine. I just haven't had any time to think about it.'

'Is it possible to leave off thinking about this here?'

Otto pulled her hand towards him, and she gave a yelp of pain. Without a doubt, the skin surrounding the bite had become more swollen and irritated than on the previous day. Sofie loosened his grip carefully and retracted her arm.

'I'll go to casualty on Monday.'

She placed one hand on each knee. Otto ran his fingers lightly around the swelling. A cross between a caress and a diagnosis.

'Casualty is open on the weekends too, you know.'

'It's a little more tender now but there isn't a red ring around it.'

'Do whatever you want, Sofie.'

On the screen, a report of a rural village where an entire mountainside had slid down. The people who lived near the landslide had fled from their houses into a tunnel. Large masses of clay blocked the tunnel entrance. Black, muddy, rocky soil. An inanimate mass that had been dangerously alive, in motion, with enormous force. The entire area would have to be secured before the rescue workers could begin digging people out of the tunnel. It was going to be a long day for the eight people trapped inside.

'I hope they managed to put on some warm clothes,' said Sofie.

'Honestly, I think they should have cancelled the dinner,' Sofie said as they sat in the taxi going towards Skøyen.

'We're finished with this,' said Otto. 'We're on our way now.'

They had been discussing at length whether or not to go to the dinner. Earlier in the day, Otto had called Ingvild to gauge the mood, and the hostess had herself been considering whether they should call it off. But in the afternoon a message arrived saying that they believed it would be good for everyone to meet on a day such as this. Ingvild had an office at the Human Rights building, on the floor beneath Otto. It was understandable that he didn't want to offend her by not coming. So Sofie had gone through her ritual of dressing and putting on make-up, though all the while something inside her resisted. They had argued. No, not argued, but Otto had said that he believed she no longer liked people. And she had replied that, well, she never had in the first place. And then she had called him a social butterfly, and that had made him a bit angry.

They peered out of the car windows, each on their own side. After a day of catastrophic television, it was almost disappointing how normal everything looked. It had stopped raining early that afternoon, but several public transport vehicles were stopped, and the taxi driver informed them that the station below the opera had been closed. Though there wasn't much traffic, he had to break now and then for barriers with warning lights where the water had scored grooves in the road. Soil and gravel was strewn across the lanes. Otherwise, there was nothing very spectacular to see before reaching Bygdøy Alley, where men in reflective vests were at work cutting large branches with chainsaws.

'Whew, it's been hard on the chestnut trees,' said Sofie and leant forward in her seat for a better view. The only thing she saw was a jumble of branches against the evening sky, which was a sickly, yellowish grey colour. The wind continued blowing heavily but the downpour was soon back at the sea from where it had come.

The other guests had all arrived, and stood in an ungainly circle within the spacious living room. Uplifted, enlightened faces. Society faces. Not surprisingly, the other guests looked somewhat older than Sofie. But she had long been familiar with being the youthful presence in social circles from the years when she had been married to Leon. That old dog, she had forgotten to tell Otto about the letter she'd received from him. Its contents were so hair-raising that she'd pushed it from her thoughts at once. Moreover, so many worse things had happened the past day. And now here she was, expected to meet four strangers she'd never before seen.

Sofie wore wrist warmers made from thin black lace. Otto had cast her a suggestive glance as she had pulled them on. Perhaps it wasn't the time of year for them, but at least they complimented her Chanel dress. The dress was of woven silk, very simple, but with a perforated expanse of black squares on the skirt. She was excessively fond of this dress which she had obtained from an online auction. Her only accessory, apart from the wrist warmers, was a tiny piece of silver jewellery with a black stone. Her dress swished and swayed cheerfully around her as she made the rounds to greet the others.

The hostess had briefly introduced the guests when they'd accepted her invitation. She had then also explained that the idea behind the gathering was for pleasant, interesting people who may not already be acquainted to have the pleasure of meeting one another. The Hopstocks, a married couple, were easy to identify. He was leisurely, distinguished, dressed like an Italian movie star. She had heavy jewellery of metal and glass around her neck and arms, and warm eyes. A colourful pair, someone might say. They lived in Drammen, he was a well-known psychoanalyst, she a textile artist. And there was also supposed to be a married couple from Høvik too, Georg and Gina. Sofie hadn't quite heard their last name. They were rich. Old

money, it emanated outward, from their eyes, their
secure smiles, you could feel it in their firm hand-
shakes, in their well-kept bodies. They donated a
lot of money to good causes, Ingvild had told her.
And then there were Maja and Henrik, whom they
had seen at a party before. He was an author, and
was always interested in talking about her father,
something which she at first had found moving and
kind. But on this particular evening it was not especially alluring to wade around through old stories.
Maja was more buoyant, sweet and down-to-earth.
She worked in the healthcare sector, and Sofie
thought about how typical it was that she had
never asked Maja about her job, whereas there was
always so much talk about what her husband was
working on. Otto had taunted Sofie that she spent
her entire life moving in social circles in which it
was unusual to meet people with completely normal jobs. And he was right in a way, though he may
not have realized that this now also involved him.

Otto's friends were psychologists, journalists,
lawyers. They had a frightening amount of knowl-
edge about human rights, about freedom of speech,
and about the political circumstances in countries
near and far. They abbreviated the names of political organizations so naturally that no one dared
ask what the abbreviations stood for. Here, Sofie
was an exciting element in the conversation,
because there was usually always some debate or
other around art museums, not least the one in

which she worked. These people listened to the radio, watched TV and read newspapers; one could get the impression that they read every single newspaper and heard all of the debate shows, it was a wonder they found time for anything else. When they asked for her perspective on a controversy surrounding an artist or a museum and leant forward with expressions of interest, Sofie would turn shy and silent. Things that were hot topics in her profession seemed so trite compared to the other discussions. What were personal conflicts and arguments about aesthetics compared to these questions of life and death?

In Sofie's social network, Otto was the exotic element. He was that good person at Tøyen. He was the one who was taking care of the Romani peoples' problems. A man who spent all of his time on the nation's bad conscience. He ensured that the problems were being attended to, and in this way exonerated them all. Otto was living proof that society was doing its share. But the best thing was that, in addition, he could converse easily about anything between earth and heaven. People were always relieved to discover that they wouldn't be required to discuss misery the entire evening.

This evening the conversation veered naturally towards the bad weather deep into the main course. A large platter was sent around the table, light veal, artfully arranged vegetables. It made the rounds several times, Sofie helped herself cautiously. The meat was pale pink inside, perfectly cooked, but she often had problems eating meat. She had a psychoanalyst for her table-mate. Lasse Hopstock spoke much and with pleasure. He expounded animatedly and with large hand gestures about what the Drammen River had looked like when he and his wife had decided to take the car to Oslo earlier that evening. The road alongside the wide river was impassable, and he illustrated how the water had come all the way up to the first story window of the central library. His long fingers danced across the table, and Sofie couldn't keep from thinking about spider legs. This man confused her. He was eloquent and funny. But there was something about the way that he posed questions, an intrusive intimacy, and then there were these unnaturally long fingers and his fluttering, grey hair. Sofie had had her fill of conceited older men who viewed themselves as casanovas. Perhaps it was wrong of her to judge all middle-aged men with artsy hairstyles. Still, she made several attempts to engage in conversation with her other table-mate. Georg sat bent forward most of the time, in discussion with Otto and Ingvild on the opposite side of the table.

'But,' Sofie heard him say, 'why include someone in society who wishes to live on its periphery?' She tried to break in to the conversation but none of them noticed her input. Otto voiced his plans about a cultural centre for the Romani people in the old military encampment at Skar in Maridalen, an idea that he was currently testing out on anyone he came across.

Suddenly, Lasse laid a hand over hers. Or, more precisely, over her wrist warmers. She flinched.

'The woman in black,' he said, trying to fix her gaze. 'The mystical, black-clad woman.'

He doesn't know, thought Sofie, amazed. They don't know. She let her eyes wander down the table. Hadn't Ingvild told the other guests anything? Sofie suddenly realized how she had become used to other people knowing about her loss, and thereby taking care.

'So, you woman in black, what is it you're hiding?' Lasse's voice was so soft that she guessed no one else at the table had heard. And still she was embarrassed on his behalf. That he could talk like that. Couldn't he hear himself?

'A tick bite,' she said quietly and pulled her hand back.

'A tick bite, really? Let me see.'

She shook her head.

'That's why I put these on,' she said, turning her wrists. 'So that people don't have to see it.'

'I'm a doctor, you know. It's a good idea to let someone look at that.'

Never, thought Sofie. I will never remove my clothing for you, even if it's only a pair of wrist warmers.

'I have an appointment with my doctor on Monday,' she said.

'Hm. I think there's still something you're hiding. You are a fathomless type. Still waters and so on. I could see it at once when you came in. I can tell if someone is carrying secrets. And sorrows. What is your secret, Sofie?'

Sofie could feel her forehead tingling. She had played this parlour game before. The gentleman asks what you're hiding. The gentleman tells you what you're actually thinking. The gentleman thinks you look sad. And then he suggests that you smile, let down your hair.

'What are those two whispering about?' Ingvild broke in. Sofie sent the hostess a thankful look.

'Catastrophe and death,' she let herself say.

'Ugh,' said Ingvild.

'Well, isn't this certainly the right day to talk about things like that?'

It was Lasse's wife. She had been quiet during the meal, now she leant over the table so that part of her heavy necklace landed on her plate.

'So you think we've talked too little about the catastrophe, Torill?'

Sofie detected a derogatory tone in his voice, something which Torill obviously also noted. She didn't respond, merely held his gaze. The other conversations around the table quieted, and the guests began fumbling with their napkins and shifting their glasses.

'Fortunately, there weren't as many casualties as was first believed,' said Ingvild, sort of shaking herself. Lasse ignored her.

'We all know that this other talk is just noise, we chat to cover up,' he said rolling his head slightly. It could seem as though he had a tight neck muscle.

'In order to forget, for this brief period of time, that we are afraid. This is what we humans are programmed for. The fear of death is what causes us to downplay danger, deny the obvious, adjust our perceptions about what is natural, and what is right. What we really want is simply to have a nice time. To be satisfied and happy. So the turn that this conversation has taken, Torill, it's classic. We are completely normal.'

His wife had leant back in her chair again. She didn't say anything. Sofie saw a bit of sauce dangling from her necklace. Now Otto jumped in:

'So you think that it's in our genes? That we deny dangers, for example, climate change, that this is part of our nature?'

'Yes. We're no better than that. We are used to thinking of humans as a well developed species, we see ourselves as nearly perfect, but the truth is that we are lacking. Evolution happens slowly. Humankind has not adapted to the enormous challenges that now face us as a species. So we react by altering our perception of the situation instead of altering our behaviour. We convince ourselves and others that it's not so dangerous. Just think about the Nazism in Germany, what kind of shift must have occurred beneath the national skin there just before and during the war. That which would have been unimaginable for many at the start—after a while became a matter of fact.'

'We do adapt,' said Sofie, almost whispering. 'We will soon come to accept that human life will be lost each time there's bad weather.'

'They haven't been able to dig out those eight people from the tunnel yet,' Georg stated. He had tasked himself with checking his mobile phone and coming up with updates.

'Precisely.' Lasse turned his head towards Sofie by popping his neck. He was a very self-confident man. His facial expression was mildly humorous.

'In situations like this, our ability to adapt can become our curse.'

'That is an extremely defeatist point of view,' said Georg.

'Perhaps, if it is a point of view. But what if we look at it as a simple explanation of the situation?'

'Then we may as well give up,' said Torill.

Lasse let his gaze wander slowly towards his wife.

'That is what we, de facto, have done.'

'Yes, these are strange times,' said Gunnar in an attempt to lighten up the mood. Which only helped somewhat, so that Ingvild stood and began to clear the table. Torill signalled that she was going outside to smoke. Lasse was one of those who followed her out to the veranda. It was as though half of the furniture disappeared with them. It became easier to breathe. Sofie walked over and sat down on the chair that had opened up between Otto and Henrik. Better to exchange a round of anecdotes from the literary life than to sit in the firing range between the psychiatrist and his wife. Otto patted her on the knee.

'Everything OK?'

'Sure,' she said. 'But my table-mate is very exhausting,' she was able to push out between her teeth.

'Oh? It looked like you were having a pleasant time.'

'One sees what one believes one sees.' Sofie leant towards him and whispered into his ear. 'Can we leave soon?'

'We've only just eaten dinner,' mumbled Otto.

For the last half an hour he had been engaged in a technical discussion and was ready to loosen his collar. Now he felt guilty for not paying more attention to Sofie. He tried to get a glimpse of Lasse out on the veranda and could just barely see his tall, lanky figure behind an ornamental bush. The wind tore the embers from his cigarette. He seemed quite charming, perhaps something of a know-it-all, but Otto had the impression that women enjoy falling for men like that. The guy couldn't really be so awful that they needed to leave the party? He looked inquiringly at Sofie, who shrugged her shoulders. She realized that it would be impossible for them to leave so soon. For a while she sat talking with Henrik, who asked how things were going with her father. Fine, she said, and pictured him with the garden hose, easily angered, stooped and frail. When she didn't say more, Henrik extracted the old story about the time that editor Krohg had taken a rejected author with him to a conciliatory dinner at the Theatre Cafe, and in the course of a humid evening cooked up a story that they were both sure would become a best seller, and which they had naturally both forgotten the next day. Sofie listened with half an ear. What is it with people? she thought. Doesn't he know that I've heard this story before? Not that it's especially funny, either. She quelled a yawn. Fortunately the dessert was on its way to the table and Gunnar, who had been on the veranda together with the Hopstock couple, said that they should go ahead and start eating, because there was apparently an argument underway outside.

'They always argue at parties, the two of them,' said Gina.

The hostess, who had seated herself in Sofie's old place, confirmed what Gina had said with an apologetic smile and said, 'Bon appétit'. The guests competed in praising the dessert, which was passion fruit and white chocolate. The Hopstocks returned again after a while. They took their places quietly. No one spoke until Lasse Hopstock tapped a spoon against his glass and stood.

'You may believe I'm about to praise the food,' he began. 'And for good reason, because this meal was a feast. The veal was beautiful. But what I actually wish to share with all of you, my friends, old and new, is that Torill, who I have been happy to call my wife for well over thirty years, has just informed me this evening that she is leaving me. We are getting divorced.'

It was as though the air in the room was suddenly expended. Sofie worked at pushing oxygen into her lungs without it sounding like a gasp.

'I was just informed about this a few minutes ago, and I dare say that it came as a surprise to me. Yes, we argue a good deal, it's not the first time that Torill has threatened to leave me. So why should I take her seriously this time? Because Torill has told me that it's serious, that she's had enough, that she's made up her mind. And so I must believe it. You look so frightened, Torill, didn't you think I would take you seriously? Don't you think we should tell our friends about the decision we've just made?'

Sofie glanced cautiously over at Torill. Her face was expressionless where she sat regarding the tabletop.

'Now cut it out, Lasse.' Gunnar sat next to Torill. He tried to look authoritative in a friendly manner.

'Yes, it's enough now. We've got the point.' Georg got up and patted Lasse lightly on the shoulders, and then it began to look as though he was putting weight on his hands, trying to press him down into the chair. But Lasse twisted away. He appeared almost cheerful.

'So, aren't you all interested to hear why Torill is leaving me? Aren't you the least bit curious?'

'No, Lasse, we aren't. Not at all,' said Ingvild. 'This is completely unnecessary. Let's stop here.'

But Lasse Hopstock wasn't about to give up yet.

'You all know, or not all of you actually, we have met some new and very pleasant people here today, but those who know us, are at least aware, that Torill is jealous. Frightfully jealous. She thinks that I flirt with every woman I meet. And tonight it was the beautiful Sofie with whom she thinks I've been flirting.'

Everyone looked at Sofie. Her legs and forehead tingled. She could feel more than she saw the tension forming in Otto's body.

'Let's assume that perhaps I was flirting with Sofie. A beautiful, intelligent woman, nothing is more natural than for a man to flirt with a beautiful, intelligent woman. But this is my enormous crime. I let myself be charmed, by a woman, by life, perhaps I drink too much, a cup overflows, a marriage ends. And perhaps it's just as well. What do you say, dear friends? I would so much like to hear other perspectives on this.'

Lasse lifted his wine glass and cast a challenging gaze out across the table.

'Isn't there anyone who would like to toast to the brave decision that Torill has taken this evening? Nora is on her way to the door, everyone! Applause! Isn't there anyone who intends to toast to it? Well, well. How should I interpret this?'

'Sit down, Lasse, and we can toast.' Georg pulled on his sleeve.

Lasse stood for a while leaning on his chair, looked as though he were searching for words, and then sat down and took a spoonful of dessert. He continued eating in a joyless manner, like a young boy forced to stay at the table until he'd finished his food. For a while, the only sound was the clinking of his spoon. The atmosphere around the table was expectant. What now? Was it still possible to act as though nothing had happened?

It was on Sofie's face that the shame was ablaze. She hadn't participated in this alleged flirting, did anyone believe that? She couldn't even bring herself to glance over at Otto. Instead she summoned her courage to look at Torill. She sat speaking quietly with Gunnar. She felt Otto lean over to her, close to her ear.

'Don't worry about it.'

Sofie turned towards him and raised her eyebrows as high as she could. And then the hostess came over, wedged herself between both of them, one hand on Sofie's shoulder, the other on Otto's.

Her sweet perfume mingled with the sour breath of wine.

'I'm sorry, Sofie, that you were exposed to this. It's not the first time that it . . . you shouldn't take it personally, please.'

Sofie suppressed a desire to ask why in heaven's name they invited people like that. Or what had made Ingvild believe that it would be interesting for her and Otto to meet these people. She was really at a loss to understand. But a polite upbringing had been embedded in her backbone, and with Otto's warm hand on her knee she was safely anchored in place. Someone spilt a wine glass, there was laughter, coffee was served in paper-thin porcelain cups. Time is a river, and the evening flowed on.

In the taxi, Sofie leant her head back on the seat and exhaled.

'It will be nice to go home now,' said Otto, taking her hand.

'How is it possible to be so intelligent and at the same time so self-absorbed?' said Sofie.

'Like that man? No, that was quite exceptional. Won't this be a terrific story to tell your friends? Or for entertaining at work?'

Your friends. Entertainment.

'Didn't you see it? That when we were leaving, and I went to shake his hand, even though it took a lot for me to do so, he tried putting his arms around me? He held onto me tightly, Otto, forced me into an embrace!'

'He was first and foremost pathetic. What I saw was a frightened, little man. He behaved like a neglected child.'

'Must men always defend other men? Is that a rule?'

Otto was quiet for a minute. The rumbling of the diesel motor permeated their bodies. There was a potent smell, the leather seats must be brand new.

'What do you think I should have done, then?' His voice had taken on a sharp tone. 'You think I should have stood up and defended you? Maybe knocked him down? Would that have salvaged the party?'

'Oh, don't be stupid.'

She turned and looked out of the side window, so that he wouldn't see her tears. Frogner Park slumbered green-black behind the gates. Inside, Vigeland's statue lived out his long, patient life in stone, would outlive them all.

'Can't we just shake it off and try to think about it as a good story?' his voice sounded behind her back. She wiped away the tears discretely with one finger before turning back around.

'Maybe I'll see it in a different light tomorrow,' she said. 'But what you said about going to the cabin, did you mean that?'

'I mostly brought it up as an excuse for going home early. But maybe we should take a trip down there to see that everything is OK? In any case, we could use some fresh air.'

'Mm-hm.'

She curled up into his side, mumbled something into his tweed jacket.

'What did you say, Sofie?'

But Sofie didn't say anything else, and as they drove towards the eastern quarter of the city, she fell asleep.

SUNDAY

That old Sunday feeling of childhood came over Otto with unexpected force as he packed the bread and spreads. In his childhood, Sundays had been synonymous with road trips. At least, when the weather permitted. And in his memory, the weather had always been good when Sunday had rolled around. The sky always just as shiny clean as the car which his father spent many hours washing and polishing each Saturday. Their white Volkswagen had been an ornament that they'd displayed on the weekend. Otto could still feel it in his body, the sputtering when the car crawled up over hilltops or around bends. That was before roads had been straightened and carved out, in those days roads comprised the tops of hills and swings, and behind the hilltops and the swings, new landscapes and views appeared, seemingly new and unfamiliar each time. Valleys in which small, glittering rivers carved a path, paddocks with horses, old stone bridges, farms so close to the roadside that you risked running down a hen or a yapping dog. Nowadays, roads were no more than a conveyor belt between two points, and Otto had certainly never polished a car. He hadn't even bothered to check that their car wasn't damaged from the storm, where it sat parked on the street. He distractedly searched for a bag of coffee and placed it in the basket.

'We have coffee down there.'

Sofie was standing directly behind him. A subtle, secret aroma from the shower accompanied her, a new lotion perhaps. Otto liked her smells, but not that she changed them so often. He placed the bag back in the cupboard.

The car's hood and windscreen were smattered with mud, leaves and other debris from the trees. Sofie arranged the basket in the back seat and herself in the passenger seat.

'You can drive. I drank more than you yesterday,' she said, fastening her seatbelt. 'Out of sheer necessity,' she added.

'Do you know what I think is strange?' asked Otto as he put the key into the ignition. 'That you, who are otherwise so particular about aesthetics, don't give a damn about how the car looks.'

'And who says I don't give a damn?'

'It obviously doesn't phase you at all that it looks like a rubbish heap, like now. You are never the one who takes care of washing the car and such things.'

'Am I not? And who do you suppose last washed the car?'

'Since you ask . . . it must have been you?'

'Yes. It was at the cabin. You sat there, your nose in your documents, and I surprised you with the hose. You got quite angry, because a bit of water splashed on your papers. I was, in fact, washing the car in that moment. But you don't seem to have noticed that.'

'OK, so you washed it last. But how often do you clean out the inside?'

On this point, he got the last laugh. But did he feel happy about it? They had woken up with the news that all of the eight people trapped inside the tunnel were feared dead. Something had gone terribly wrong during the rescue attempt. They had simply listened to the news, not a single word in comment. The car rolled slowly through Jens Bjelkes Gata. The sun peeked out and the city was beginning to dry. As with darkness, normality was always present, ready to fill every cranny.

When Sofie and Otto had come to Tøyen, they had felt like settlers. Their move was to be a recovery. They would resurrect themselves on another turf. But it was also about something more, something larger than themselves. This was the new Norway. This was the real Oslo. By living here, they participated in real life, not in an illusory life, not in a life of facades, they could now stop playing the daily game of be-happy, that's what they'd said. It had been a demonstration—they moved from the neighbourhood where the mass murderer had lived and became a part of everything that the murderer had hated and feared. It had been the right thing to do, what they did. But what now? That good feeling they had shared, the feeling of arm-wrestling with fate, was starting to fade together with the neighbourhood. All around them things became worn, year after year. Streets full of pot-holes, buildings peeling paint, parks overgrown and heaped with rubbish.

Their mood lightened as they drove out onto the E18. Where flat, straight roads unrolled before them, and a very promising sky up above. A thin layer of morning fog was returning, and the sun began to take hold. It was as if the storm belonged to another era.

'There's something . . . I saw that there was a letter on your desk. From Leon?'

'Yes, that's true. I meant to tell you. He's getting married again.'

'But he didn't send you a wedding invitation?' Otto's voice sounded terrified.

'No, no, my God. He just wanted to inform me. And guess what?'

'Oh, no. Not with another student?'

'Yep. She's twenty-two.'

Otto whistled.

'Which means she's as old as I was when I met him.'

'And not only that . . .' Otto kept his eyes trained on a point far out in front of the car.

'No,' said Sofie quietly.

'She is younger than Marie would have been.'

'Yes.'

'By two years.'

'Yes.'

Sofie sat fiddling with something. Her nails, or a thread in her trousers. Her hair fell forward, hiding her face. Otto knew that the wrong comment could make her withdraw completely.

'He must be almost seventy now,' he ventured.

'He'll be seventy in October. He's celebrating with the wedding. Just imagine, that this man, with grey hair and beard and an artificial hip and another that will have to be replaced soon—he's begun using a cane!—that this man has managed to lure a young, Chinese student to Vienna on God-only-knows-what premises.'

'Is the girl from China?'

'Yes. He says himself that they had a totally special connection at a seminar in Beijing. So now he's sort of saved the poor girl from her People's Republic, from the clutches of her strict parents who were to decide with whom she should be married, and he's tugged on every string and exploited every one of his fine titles for all they're worth, it's apparently been a real drama. On top of all of this, he's taken her maidenhead and now feels that he's a real hero for marrying the girl.'

'Taken her maidenhead? Seriously, Sofie. Did he write that to you?'

'Yes, you have to read the letter, it's so revealing that you won't be able to believe it.'

'But why does he tell you all of this?'

She wrinkled her forehead. 'Now, that's a good question.'

'That's actually the most interesting thing here. Isn't it, to put it mildly, strange that he informs you about whose maidenhead he's taken, and who he plans to marry, for that matter?'

'No, Otto . . . Yes, it is a bit strange. The way that he does it. He writes as though he takes it for granted that I would like to share his joy.'

'He is not so dumb as to think that you would be happy that he's marrying a girl who's two years younger than his daughter would have been?'

'Maybe he thinks he's doing something heroic and good, and wants to prove to me that isn't just a bag of shit?'

Otto sniffed, but didn't say any more. He must tread carefully here. He couldn't mention exactly how revolting he found Sofie's ex-husband, because that would be to criticize her, to show contempt for her previous life.

'He simply must not have considered how this looks to you,' he finally said.

'I don't know,' said Sofie. 'I actually have no idea what he was thinking.'

'Does he ever think about Marie?'

'Yes. He does.'

Sofie watched fields of green, yellow and black glide past on both sides. Wetness gleamed over everything. The world had washed itself.

Thoroughly, frightfully thoroughly. The Farmer would certainly not be happy about this rain. Where there were cornfields, large portions of the corn lay in bulging stripes, like wet, combed hair against the ground.

'Does he actually write that to you? That he thinks about her?'

'I don't often get letters from him, maybe only once every half year. Maybe less often.'

She didn't say more, so after a while Otto found a channel with classical music. Piano music. Springing, trilling, light. And that curious humming and grunting of Glenn Gould. They passed through the last tunnels, and Sofie rolled the window all the way down. The smell of greenery filled the car.

'Sunday excursion!' Otto exclaimed, pressing down on the gas.

Sofie loved him when he was like this. Childish, free, without his papers and feelings of responsibility and self-righteousness. And completely free of the vanities that had so much characterized Leon. It was his seriousness that she had first fallen for. His engagement, his advocacy for society's weakest members. His blue, honest eyes. Otto often expressed frustration at accomplishing so little. Sofie sometimes wondered if he longed for his old job in the law firm. Now he bore all of the defeats and the few triumphs alone. He had become grey. But that would have happened in any case, according to him.

111

Sofie stroked his neck. The fresh air would do them good. Maybe they could stay the night at the cabin, and come back to the city early enough to go to work? Driving down to the cabin was like taking a break from pain. She leant back and waited for the turmoil to quiet, aching knots to loosen up. Her stiff shoulders. The cramps in her thighs. Little by little they released their hold. It was about focusing on the positive: she could still pull fresh air down into her lungs. That doesn't go without saying.

Everything looked normal as they drove down the bumpy country road. When the cabin had become theirs, they had painted it grey like the rocky crags round about it. The one-storey cabin was situated between two low outcroppings, so well hidden that they could walk around naked if they wished. The only view was from the kitchen window and the tiny terrace outside of the kitchen, from here you could glimpse the fjord, which was only a short walk away. Otto parked, and they sat briefly without moving, enjoying the sight of their tiny paradise. This place of freedom, this little speck on the earth that they could call their own, was worth every moment of work that it would ever cost them.

'My grass,' Sofie tended to say whenever she padded barefoot out onto the dewy wet grass in the mornings. 'My earth. My straw. My bushes.'

'My rocks,' Otto might say sarcastically, clapping the mountain that both protected and shut

them out. Their cabin neighbours had incited may-
hem for an entire summer, blasting away a similar
outcropping. An excavator rumbled and a lorry
rattled back and forth for weeks, the ground trembled and the boom echoed loudly across the water
when the charge went off. Now, a massive patio lay
where the outcropping had been, and in the middle
of the enormous wood patio, the cabin neighbours
had placed a group of white plastic furniture. Sofie
and Otto agreed that it didn't look nice. It didn't
look nice, it couldn't be possible, but he believed in
his innermost thoughts that Sofie was jealous of
their fine view out over the water.

The sky above the cabin and the stone crags
had now taken on the colour of unwashed jeans,
and a light breeze rustled in some long, golden
stalks of straw that hadn't been bent by the rain.
Otto was the first to open the car door. There was
a sucking sound as he placed his foot on the
ground. A pool had formed in the middle of the
lawn. The water soaked quickly into Sofie's thin
sneakers as she tried to navigate through to the
door. She waited until Otto came behind her, with
the keys and picnic basket. He was still always
astounded at how natural it was for her to let others
carry her things, to let others drive, to unlock the
door, to wait on her hand and foot. And he was at
least just as astounded at how natural it felt for him
to do it. He unlocked the door.

The cabin door was the door into something
else, a foreign place, although they came often. This

was the one place where they could leave and come back again without anything having changed. The only place where life didn't seem to rush them or to force changes that were beyond their control. But this time something was different. Their sense of smell was the first to notice. Sofie came to a halt in the entryway and sniffed the air. It smelt like a raw cellar, like silt, mildew, wet wood. The outer door stayed open after them and let in an angled square of light. She walked inside, and because her legs were already soaked, she didn't feel it immediately. She pulled apart the curtains and could feel that they were heavy, wet on the bottom.

'Otto, there's water on the floor!'

He had been walking in the other direction, there was a sound of glass crackling.

'What the hell happened here?'

They understood soon enough. The veranda door had blown open and let in the storm. The frame swung lightly on its hinges in the draft, the glass from the door was smashed and lay strewn across the flooded floor together with twigs, leaves and grime. A large Chinese vase that had been standing near the door had toppled and rolled all the way into the living area. A piece along its rim had broken off. Sofie stood as though frozen, unable to take it all in at once. Everyday objects had obtained completely new places and positions. A wet tablecloth encircled the sugar bowl like a swollen squid, an old ship model lay fallen over with a cracked mast, drenched magazines had unfolded onto pages about sports and interiors, everything helter-skelter across the floor.

'We forgot to lock the door.' Her voice sounded dead in the room.

'One of us forgot to lock the door.' Otto turned towards her. 'You are the one who always has to air it out.'

'What do we have a veranda door for if not to stay open?'

'And that's fine enough, as long as you only remember to close it.'

'You are always the one who checks before we leave! You know that I'm not able to get it all the way closed again.'

Sofie picked up a swollen roll of paper towels, which crumbled to pieces in her hands and fell down on the floor with a wet slap. Anything that had been positioned on the table or benches had been swept over, most objects had ended up on the floor. Pictures hung crookedly, one lay on the floor, backside up. Sofie didn't have to check, she knew that it was ruined. One word resounded through her mind. *Ruin.* Everything looked so impoverished and wretched, all of the things that she loved so much. The treasures unearthed at the flea market, gifts from friends, things that she had from home when she was a child. She tried to imagine how it must have been when the door had blown open and the wind barged in at its worst. Like the inside of a dishwasher, maybe.

Otto stepped into the living room, where everything that had been loose now lay scattered between the two walls and the rug on the floor was dark with water. Sofie followed behind, picking up a paper that had been stuck to the floor. The ink had spread outwards. She crumpled the paper together. In one corner lay a lampshade. She lifted it up and screamed.

'A frog!'

The grey-brown creature sat completely still, but she could see his breaths. There was also a flitting movement in his yellow, bulging eyes. She placed the lampshade over him again.

'I have to find something to capture that beast.'

'Can't you just pick it up with your hands?'

Sofie hesitated. Otto walked over and took away the shade. The frog leapt over his feet and began hopping in a panic around the room. Its back legs were enormously long.

'You scared him!'

'That wasn't really my intention. I wanted to help him. Maybe you could get the lampshade again?'

At last, the frog was outside.

'You can fix the door,' said Otto.

'How do you imagine that I should do it?'

'Well, you could probably find some kind of material out in the shed that you can use to secure the door. The most important thing is that it can be shut securely.'

Sofie looked at him furiously. 'Why should I do it, when you are the one who knows how to do it? Is it because you think that the whole thing is my fault?'

'No, it's more that it was a continuation of our conversation just now. It's like it's always an assumption that the car and anything technical or practical at home and at the cabin is my job. Now we have the chance to switch rolls a little.'

'This is just ridiculous, Otto. If it was a handy-woman that you wanted, you should have married a handy-woman.'

'OK. Then you start cleaning and washing and I'll see if I can board up the door.'

Sofie made a face behind his back as he walked out into the entryway to put on boots. It was a mild expression for the rage that she felt. She punched her hand hard against the doorframe as she came into the bedroom. Inside, it was as if the ocean had come for a visit and left behind the smell of rotten seaweed. Everything was where it usually was, except it all seemed wet and dank, the bedding, all of the clothes inside the wardrobe. Sofie looked at her sore knuckles as she pulled out her work clothes, a pair of shorts and an unwashed T-shirt. The clothes were sticky to pull on.

In the living room, she stood looking at the large rug, it would have to go outside. There was no way she could ask Otto for help. She carried all of the furniture out to the lawn and began to tug and pull on the rug. It was like a dead corpse. She dragged it through the hall and across the lawn and was able to get it up the hill to dry. The fine pouffe made of sheep's wool had attempted to soak up all of the water on its own. It looked like a grey stone, and was nearly as heavy. She heard herself grunt as she lifted, pulled and carried. The sun met her eyes with blazing arrows. On the last day of their vacation, there had also been sunshine and warmth. How was it, then, with that door? It had most likely stood open, held by the hook. But in the afternoon they had gone down to swim, and they must have shut it before leaving for the beach. And afterwards they'd gone straight home, hadn't they? Sofie closed her eyes against the sun and straightened her back. Otto was not allowed to pass the blame on her like that. She could hear him banging around in the shed. Suddenly something crashed inside. And then a long string of cursing.

Otto stood there looking at the fishing poles and nets that had tumbled down the wall as he had tried to pry out a board. The thin wooden floor was built directly above the ground, and it smelt like earth. His head nearly touched the roof, and he had to creep around to avoid the fat, black spiders hanging from the corners. It felt as though something were creeping and crawling over his entire body. They should have done something with this shed ages ago.

He sighed and began to pile the things that had fallen. Sweat dripped into his eyes, his movements were hard and abrupt. His head was busy formulating the wording for a text message. It was important to find the right words, the right tone. He had basically reached a clear decision now, but dreaded typing it in. It was to Karin. The contact between them completely bordered on inappropriate. Sofie would have considered it far beyond. If she had reacted so strongly to him speaking with Karin at the exhibit opening, how outraged would she be to know about the texting, the phone conversations? Not to talk about what had happened behind the cabin last summer, while she had been preparing supper. As he had stood with the sounds of the kitchen in his ears—Sofie chopping herbs—as he trailed his hands down along Karin's back, pulling her into him. It had been madness. Pure madness. What had started as a friendly, comforting hug had become too . . . he resisted the word. Well, too erotic. Their embrace hadn't lasted many seconds, half a minute at the most, but it had nonetheless lasted too long. It had set something in motion. And there was some indication that Karin had read more into it than he did.

There was no other way out. The words had seemed reasonable when he'd configured them in his head, but when he typed them in on the lit panel, they looked cowardly and phoney. She has no limits, he thought. No constraints. He was the one who had to set limits. He swapped out a couple of words and pressed *Send*.

When he finally emerged from the shed with a few thin slabs and a long board, the terrace had been covered with objects, and the furniture littered the entire yard. It looked as though they were having a garage sale. Sofie was hanging out their clothes too, in the hope that they would smell like wind and sun before evening came. They looked cheap where they hung.

Inside the cabin, Sofie first swept up the shards of glass. Then she went around with a large garbage bag and filled it with everything that couldn't be salvaged. She decided to try saving the old salt and pepper shakers that had been on the kitchen counter. They were so cute, two penguins with small leather wings. The wings had been soaked, and inside there was nothing but black and white paste. What a mess! Sofie rested her head against the kitchen cupboard. It was as though a door was swinging back and forth in her head, out towards the light, in towards the dark. Swish, swish. Light, dark. Light, dark. What is the point, she thought. Clean up, straighten out, smooth over. Only for the illusion of comfort, of peace?

By the time she was finally ready to clean up the water, Otto had begun with the door. First he nailed the frame firmly into the doorway. He looked at Sofie as he did it, as if to say: There. Now there won't be any airing out for a while. And then he started nailing on slabs and boards. It turned half-dark inside, as gloomy as in the forest. As in a trance, Sofie dragged the mop through the mud and water, twist and drag, twist and drag. The bucket became full, and she was about to stand to go outside and empty it. As she lifted her gaze, she was looking straight at two legs. She knew at once, they were *his* legs. The dirty field boots. The chequered reflective tape he had stuck around his pant legs. And the rifle. A Ruger Mini-14. The name of the weapon was one of the things that had been burnt into her memory. Ruger Mini-14. It was a strange sound in her ears, a kind of low, rumbling hum. She looked down at the floor again, and when she looked back up, it was gone. The hum was gone too, other sounds had returned. Otto hammering and banging outside, music streaming out from the radio. Sofie drew her breath deeply a few times and stood up carefully. Her knees hurt. She realized that she'd had a kind of hallucination, and was more astonished than afraid. So many years that she'd been waiting for her daughter to appear to her. In a dream, in a vision, or simply as the presence that many speak of. One woman at her bereavement support group had found comfort from knowing that her son had become one with nature, she found comfort in the forest, talking with the small birds. Another had told that she found a connection at the gravesite, she was able to have long conversations there. Others felt the presence in special rooms, in special places. Sofie had never felt such a presence. There was only silence from Marie. Her girl was only completely and terribly gone. And now *he* came. Sofie grabbed hold of the bucket and walked slowly out, carefully, as though something might break, as though she were an old woman.

It was late in the day when they finally opened the picnic basket. There was no longer room for them on the terrace, and inside the cabin, the fan heater roared at full blast. When Sofie came out with the coffee, Otto had placed himself in the armchair, which stood outside so that the bottom ruffle could dry out in the sun. Sofie pulled over a small table and sat down on the doorstep.

'How serious is the damage?' she asked. It was the first time that either of them had spoken for several hours, and the words hovered, flapping in the air, ready to be answered or shot down.

'In pounds and pence?'

'Yes, or in hours of work.'

'We won't be able to fix this ourselves. I've managed to get the door shut somewhat, so now we can only hope that we're able to convince the glazier to come out here as soon as possible.'

'In pounds and pence then.'

'No idea.'

Otto looked almost content where he sat, squinting at the sun, his coffee cup propped against his stomach. The sky above them was like a painting, the clouds were white and so light that it looked as though they had been rubbed outwards with a sponge. They had kicked off their boots, Otto sat wearing only his boxer shorts and undershirt. It was hard to believe that another storm was on its way soon, as powerful as the last one, but that's what they had said over the radio as Sofie was down on all fours drying the floors. Another early autumnal storm was expected across the country during the week. Light, dark. Light, dark. Suddenly it came over her, an intense need to be carefree, to be nothing but happy. She was always the one who had to ruin the mood.

'Another storm is coming. Towards the weekend, maybe earlier.'

'You're joking.'

'The meteorologists said. And now even the politicians are worried.'

'Then I will need to secure the door even better. Those planks won't hold for long.'

'But if the carpenter . . . '

'The glazier. We don't know if we can get anyone to come out on such short notice.'

The air was once again filled with disquiet. The sun scorched their faces, and Sofie felt the drops of sweat trickle down her spine, vanishing into her shorts. But from the ground, a creeping cold made its way through her sneakers and up her legs. She had hoped that they could stay the night at the cabin, now her heart skipped a beat when he said that they would have to keep the fan heater on overnight.

'So, we have to stay here?' she said.

'Isn't that what you wanted?'

Gurgling, bubbling sounds. The ground beneath them was alive. Millions of organisms in motion down there in the dark, cleaning up, or just keeping things going. They never stopped, always kept at work.

'What you wanted. That sounds like a book title,' Sofie said finally.

'Yes. A typical Norwegian novel,' said Otto.

'About everything that you ever hoped for . . . '

' . . . and how things have actually turned out.'

'A typical life,' said Sofie.

'And a typical novel,' said Otto.

Sofie looked down at her right hand. Opened and shut her fist several times. The hand with the tick bite had swollen up and it felt numb and stiff. Not so strange, she had been sticking her hands into dirty water the entire day. She should have used rubber gloves.

'The more I think about it,' stated Otto. '*Hunger* was the optimal book title at the end of the 1800s. It should have been followed up with the big Norwegian novel *Stuffed* towards the end of the next century. What ever happened to that novel?'

'Well, we did have *The Conquerors*,' said Sofie, looking up.

'*The Conquerors*, yes, that's just as good. And soon someone is going to follow up with the novel *The Scream*.'

'Maybe I'm the one who should write that.'

The nearly imperceptible break in her voice. Otto had to give himself a little push to get up out of the arm chair. He sat on the doorstep, placed his arm around her. Gave a squeeze. She sank into him, soft and rigid at the same time. He could feel that steel coil. Her backbone that continued to hold and uphold.

'We'll stay here tonight,' he said. 'We can build a fire down at the beach. It will be a nice evening.'

'What you want,' said Sofie.

'What you want,' said Otto, 'is what *we* want, right now.'

'Celestial body,' said Sofie. 'Now I get it.'

'What do you get?'

The moon was on its way up. A sliver that showed above the ocean's surface, shimmering, pulsing.

'That old phrase. That they used to call it a body. It looks like a living form there, clambering over the edge.'

It was cloudless and alarmingly quiet, their cabin neighbours had returned home, the two of them were the only audience in this infinite hall. The beach nearest the cabin was a small cove with a narrow strip of white, fine-grained sand strewn with dark, round stones. The sky had drawn a blue-violet curtain in front of which the moon glided upwards, at first absurdly large and blood-orange-coloured, in a slow butoh dance. Just as it seemed that he was about to come rolling across the water's surface towards them, he ascended—for a moment it seemed as though he hung connected to the fjord but then, with an almost audible, soft burst, he detached and swayed freely skyward. Filled himself out fully, but now with a less fright-ening marigold colour.

They sat on a flat stone that had stored up the sun's warmth. Before them in the sand, a small fire glowed. They were finished doing what they could at the cabin. In the afternoon, Otto had decided that he must secure the door better, so he had driven to the nearest petrol station. In addition to a few rolls of thick plastic, he had returned with a package of sausages for grilling, which they now skewered and held above the embers.

'It's almost scary,' said Sofie.

'What? The moon?'

'Yes, not only that, but that it's so quiet. I don't think I've heard a single bird tonight, not the entire afternoon. The air is so heavy. And the colours are so intense. It's just before the storm.'

'But the storm isn't supposed to come yet, is it?'

She stared at the forest behind them. The reddish-yellow light from the moon and the lit-up flickers from the fire made the trees dance. Dark green shadows stole in and out between the trunks. Around them, the beach glowed a pale, burnt colour. The stones could have been the skin of an ill-fated person, buried beneath the sand.

'Dante's Inferno,' she said without further explanation.

'Yes, something is roiling up there.'

Otto had been looking at the fire, he turned and flipped the grilling stick, he didn't see what Sofie saw. She began eating her sausage and discovered too late that it was completely cold on one end. She threw the stick and half of the sausage into the fire.'

'Sofie.' Otto looked at her disapprovingly.

'Oh.' She hid her face in her hands. 'I'm just so terribly exhausted.'

'You're famished, that's what you are. Look, you can have mine.'

'I can't stand sausages.'

'That's what we have. Sofie, you're not allowed to stop eating. You've become thinner again lately.'

She lifted her head and looked at him.

'It's true. You've eaten less and less. You say that you're starving and then you leave your plate full of food, and you've only eaten a tiny bit.'

'I'm completely normal. I haven't really got thinner, have I?'

'It's strange you don't notice it yourself. It's quite apparent to me. You're not allowed to become as thin as you were.'

Sofie took the sausage that he had been holding in front of her. He skewered a new one and poked the fire. Sparks flew upwards, extinguished, and lived anew as small, nearly invisible flakes of ash, settled on hair and clothes or found rest in the cool sand.

'I can't stop thinking about this ex-husband of yours.'

'Ugh, is he going to be allowed to disturb us here, too?'

Sofie had devoured the sausage almost without noticing it. She could now feel her hunger very strongly, and she tried to fish the grill stick out of the fire.

'Sorry,' said Otto. 'But after what you told me in the car, he keeps popping into my head all the time, like one of those cabaret figures who never stops. With a hat and cane.'

'You've seen him at his worst, at his most self-pitying moment. He was awful at the funeral.'

'Yes, he was.'

Sofie burnt her fingers and had to give up trying to reach the stick. Otto handed her another grilled sausage, which she took and immediately began eating. Doesn't she notice how hot it is? thought Otto.

No, the cabaret figure had begun to sing and dance for her as well. Or, perhaps more correctly, to cough, sniff and whine. And writhe around on the church bench. Sofie remembered very little from the funeral, but she could recall his sounds and gestures. He had stumbled in just before the ceremony began and caused a scene because he hadn't any money to pay the taxi. Judit had jumped up and gone out to settle for him. The clock had begun to chime while she was outside. Leon was able to squeeze himself into the bench behind Sofie. Her neck was stiff. She wanted to scream out loud when he leant forward to explain that he hadn't had time to take out Norwegian money. But Otto stopped him. She remembered this too. How Otto had held her hands then, lightly, but not too lightly. How he had tried to make space for her in a room so full of others' sorrow and others' needs that there was nearly no air left over for Sofie to breathe, no space for a single movement. How could their sorrow be larger and take up more space than hers?

Otto studied her sharp, clean profile in the firelight. There were sides of her that he'd never understood. And the biggest puzzle of all was how this cautious, discerning woman could fall for someone like Leon. He looked a bit younger and less helpless in the photos in Sofie's old albums. Otto had only looked at these albums a few times. The photographs gave him a deeply unsettled feeling. He saw a woman who looked like his wife, but her smile was different, and her head was cocked flirtatiously. She no longer cocked her head flirtatiously, she no longer gave the world that teasing glance. She said it herself too. That the photo belonged to another life. That she was someone else then. A completely different person, that's how she had said it.

Maybe she was more beautiful now than in those old photos. But she no longer radiated light, not in the same way. She used to be the life of the party, the one who thought up antics, the one who was certain of sunshine, even when rain was predicted. Now it was his job to lighten things up, uplift. Otto looked at her, she was looking at the moon. She noticed his gaze.

'It was Munch who came up with the moonbeam. In several of his paintings, you don't see the moon at all, only a stripe in the water. In a way, he tethered the moon to the earth.'

Otto knew the motif well. Sofie had lived in Vienna for a period to write her thesis on *Summer Night on the Beach*, a painting with a story that had engaged her strongly. And she wasn't the only one. The literature professor, Leon Schimmert, reputedly a celebrity in the art milieu in Vienna, had published several articles on the painting, which had been a love gift for Alma Mahler, the niece of Gustav Mahler. She had chartered a relationship to the author Franz Werfel while her second husband, the architect Walter Gropius, was off fighting for Germany during the First World War. Gropius returned home on leave, bringing with him this painting, only to learn that his wife had meanwhile borne a child with another. The marriage ended but she kept the painting. During the Second World War, Alma Mahler and Franz Werfel, who was a Jew, had to flee to the USA. Alma's stepfather, who initially exchanged letters with Munch to secure some of his paintings for Vienna, sold *Summer Night on the Beach* to a Nazi-controlled gallery. Following the war, and up until 2006, the Austrian state refused to return the painting to Alma Mahler. At the time that Sofie wrote her thesis, the painting hung in the Belvedere Palace in Vienna. The way that Otto understood it, Leon had helped her to gain access and contacts, and they eventually began meeting regularly at a cafe near the gallery.

It must have been the massive accumulation of art and culture that had captivated her, thought Otto. The music swept her along with it, the intellectual *niveau*, the gorgeous buildings, the high ceilings, the exclusivity, the un-Norwegianness of talking for hours across a cafe table. Interest from an older, respected professor. Maybe he had been gallant in a way, in that clumsy, helpless manner that women seem to like. And it might have been his flat, all those rooms filled with books piled floor to ceiling. For Sofie, this was in all likelihood an alluring blend of something exotic but also familiar. The lavish and grand combined with something safe and fatherly. For what could be more natural, Otto continued in his thoughts, then that Sofie— who had been brought up by a father who spoke to her as with an adult, allowed her to leaf through books and discuss manuscripts with her before she could barely even read herself—should be drawn to this kind of older professor.

But there was something in this photo that grated on him. For when it came down to it, Leon didn't much resemble Sofie's father. Her parents had been at odds with their son-in-law almost from the first moment.

'What are you thinking about?' Sofie lay her head back, as though sunning herself in the moonlight.

'Well, what do you think? I'm thinking of you and Leon. One of the universe's great mysteries.'

Her teeth shone.

'That you could marry him. Have a child with him. Live together with him for so many years.'

'I am a simple woman.'

'I can understand that you were infatuated, seduced, besotted. But that you could love him?'

'It never came to that. You know that. The crush lasted only until I found out that he had a tendency to indulge in a young student each semester, and that he didn't plan on stopping that habit just because he had become a father. Our relationship never had time to develop into love. But I still feel a kind of fondness for him.'

Sofie sat up straight. Her voice became urgent.

'I hated his behaviour at the funeral. But he didn't know what to do with his grief. Which of us knew? And he didn't have anyone there who could help him.'

'That's where women have a blind spot. A man presents himself as helpless, and your hearts melt away and take good sense with them. He only felt sorry for himself. It didn't seem as though he spent a single thought on Marie, not a word about what she'd been through, no concern for you, it was all about him, him, him. The most trivial things, like how he had forgotten to bring a scarf and had caught a cold . . . '

'Otto, think about it. He was Marie's father. He had lost a child. He and I lost a child.'

The words that had been on their way out stuck in his throat. When he quieted, she continued in a milder tone:

'Everyone grieves in their own way. The fact that Leon didn't have much contact with Marie is partly my fault. I was the one who moved, and who took our daughter with me. She was six. It's not so strange that he was therefore unused to being a father. But he wrote such wonderful letters to her. Every letter was like a book, and he made collages with pictures that he clipped out of newspapers and magazines, and wrote small stories about an absentminded professor and all of the strange things he experienced. Marie loved these letters so much.'

'Yes, I know that. She had a lock on her drawer, it wasn't just anyone who was allowed to see what was inside. But I was able to convince her to show me some of the letters . . . '

Details. It was the details that hurt, it was in the details that the Devil sat clawing, biting, tearing asunder. Otto knew that, but he couldn't always safeguard himself, couldn't always make himself stop in time. He shouldn't have said this last part. The letters. The drawer. The lock. It was too much.

It had all been too early. Her thin, tiny hands unlocking the drawer. That thin, tiny voice reading the stories about the absentminded professor. She sat there on the bed unfolding the letters, her treasures. Told him wisely that this professor, he resembled her father *a great deal*. That sweet voice, her laughter.

They sat there quietly. The little that was said, wafted away into the evening. As the evening stretched, the moon drifted further away, colder, the moonlight white as phosphorous. The light gathered in the water like a column. The moon a blank face on a pedestal of light. The tide came in, and small lethargic tongues of water began lapping at their fire. It hissed.

'We have to go before the sea eats the ground out from under us,' said Sofie.

Otto lay a hand on her thigh, held on.

'I wonder all the time whether I was too emphatic when we discussed having children.'

'But you didn't want to.'

'That was before . . . '

He couldn't continue. Before she died. Before she was murdered. Before the horror. There was no way to say it. It was possible to say and think 'before', and it was possible to say and think 'after'. But what was in between didn't have any name. The expanse between before and after was a barren landscape they seldom approached, it was nothing but cold and empty and damp. Sofie shivered. She drew her knees up to her chin and wrapped both arms around them. The was more hissing from the fire, and then it went out.

'What is it that you're saying now, actually? That you wish that we had had children anyway?'

Her voice had taken on a somewhat hard, cold tone.

'I don't know really . . . Not after . . . afterwards. That would have been like trying to create a replacement for Marie. That's how you felt, wasn't it?'

Sofie didn't answer.

'But now I think that before . . . before we lost her, I was too stubborn in my opinion. Maybe I wasn't as resolute as I sounded, but I thought things were fine the way they were. We each had a child, they were wonderful, they were doing fine. But now I regret it so much that I didn't listen to you more then.'

Otto was prepared for another cold reply. But she turned suddenly towards him, and her voice had taken on a totally different tone, almost tender:

'You started thinking about this because you're worried about Peter. You are worried about him, aren't you?'

'Of course I am.'

'Take some time off and travel down to see him.'

She stood up stiffly from the stone and gathered the few things they'd brought with them.

Grabbed the basket, swung the blanket over her arm. In the same tone, she said, 'It's so terrible thinking that all of this is just going to continue. It would be better knowing that it will all be over soon.'

They stared at one another, but in their moonlit faces there were only dark craters. The heavens gaped. The sand slid away beneath their feet, time raged onward.

The bedding. They should have hung the bedding out to dry as well. Sofie could feel it the moment she lay down. It was damp, nearly soaked, and smelt bad. The entire cabin was filled with a sickening stench which the warm air from the heater fan had stirred up. The furniture was back inside, but the heavy wool rug hadn't dried yet, so they had left it hanging outdoors. Sofie tossed. She was so tired that her whole body itched. Or maybe it was the moisture from the bedding that made her itch. A feeble light came in from the living room, just reaching the bed. She heard Otto rummaging around in the kitchen. He hadn't said anything more about the door. The comforter lay on the floor already, now she tore off her T-shirt. The window was opened, but there was no breeze outside, the curtains hung unwavering. Wasn't Otto coming soon?

No, he wasn't. He was standing at the kitchen counter pouring a glass of water. He wondered if he should shower again. Sweat glistened on his arm. They had propped open the window, leaving the door between the living room and bedroom open for a cross breeze. But it was as though the entire cabin, and not only the veranda door, had been packaged inside thick, black plastic. He could hear Sofie tossing and turning in the room. He hoped she would be able to sleep. What she had said . . . *It would be better knowing that it will all be over soon* . . . He also didn't wish for things to continue, not everything, and not necessarily as they had been before. But to wish for everything to be over? He shouldn't read too much into it, that's just the way she was. He filled his glass once more. At least the water was refreshing.

Beyond the cabin walls it was night-time, peace. Inside the cabin, itching, turmoil. The table and chairs stood in their usual positions, yet it seemed as though things weren't in the right spot. It was impossible to go lay down in this jumble, in this disarray. If only a small breeze would blow, a soft wind through the room, to open things up, to cool and expunge. There weren't many hours before they would have to wake, clean up the last bit, find a solution for the rug. Get into the city. It struck him that he hadn't thought about his job all day. That was something, at least. Now he thought that the first thing he'd have to do was to take a trip up to Ullern to check on things there. They had been required to vacate the camp by Wednesday, but many people may already have left due to the flooding. It seemed as though the conditions were awful up there.

Otto leant against the counter, stretched out his aching back. One of the few things that he had accomplished as the leader of FROM was to nego-tiate the so-called two-week agreement. It relieved some pressure when the impoverished nomads were allowed to camp out for two weeks at a time in locations that weren't a great nuisance for the city's inhabitants. But there were a lot of opinions about what the expression 'great nuisance' entailed. So most of his time was spent ensuring that both the municipality and the campers complied with their mutual obligations. He wasn't able to get much further than that. Building up mutual respect and understanding . . . those fine words that he had tossed about when he first got the job, now drifted about without a sail or oars.

His back made a small creaking noise. He swore quietly.

Sofie was lying flat on her back, naked in the bed, listening. It had become quiet out there. Could he perhaps have gone and laid down on the sofa? Had he gone outside to lie down? Was the damp bed so intolerable, was she so intolerable? She lay thinking through what had been said throughout the evening. He hadn't seemed upset, he simply wanted a glass of water, he'd said. She heard the floorboards creaking, and then all was still again. He was making quite a fuss about Leon lately. It irritated her. She seldom spoke about his ex-wife, although there was certainly enough to say about her. But this was about Marie. Of course it was Marie. Otto had been a good stepfather. Wise, not intrusive. He had seen her in a completely different way than Sofie. That had been a big help. Where

Sofie was insecure about all that she didn't know about her daughter, and worried about every one of her character traits, Otto had said that everything was OK. It would all make sense, he had said, everything that they didn't understand would make sense later on. They never had the chance to learn if he had been right. But it had been right of him to shield Marie from the worst of Sofie's nagging and the enormous load of worries that she constantly lugged around.

Otto lay on the floor, like a ball, with his feet pulled up to his chin. He rolled back and forth, massaging his spine. He felt agitated because he hadn't received any response from the message he'd sent to Karin. She usually replied immediately. Now he repeated the words in his message, wondered if he'd been too harsh. He was not tempted to go into the bedroom. He wasn't tempted to be inside at all. Sofie was most likely wondering why he didn't come. It had been wrong to blame her for the door, but she was so inconsiderate. Waited for him to fix everything. *We* forgot, she said, and meant *him*. But it would be so dumb to let this ruin everything. A strong wind, an unlocked door, rain and broken glass in on their floor. These are details, he said to himself. It's so small. It's almost nothing.

How often did he say this? Quite often. Life was full of small catastrophes. Small mishaps. And it was stressful and troublesome, but it didn't mean anything. Not when one has been where we have been, thought Otto. What was it Sofie had said earlier that evening . . . Dante's inferno. They had been to the gate. They had peered inside. Otto stopped rolling, but remained on the floor, his arms around his knees. He must correct himself. He couldn't get past it. *She* had been the one to peer in.

Sofie was magnanimous. She had allowed him space to grieve, and had never asserted that he couldn't know, that it was impossible for him to understand. Of course, he had also grieved for her. But now she had put him in his place. *He and I lost a child*. Her voice, how coldly she had said it. He should never have gone off on Leon in that way. But then he never would have heard how she positioned him in relation to all of this. And with good reason. Every possible reason.

The Inferno. The endless, indescribable hours they had waited at the hotel. Evening, night. The young people from the island, the faces they came with, the stories they came with. And for every young person who came, there was someone who didn't come. They hadn't found Marie anywhere. They couldn't find anyone who knew who she was. For a while they held out a wild hope that she hadn't been out there at all, that she had gone behind their backs and snuck off to some other place. Somewhere where she was safe. They pulled up photos of Marie on their mobile phones. Went around showing them, asking whether anyone had seen her. All the while, people kept streaming in.

Relatives, friends. Everywhere people who cried, hugged one another, and people searching, just as they were. In the end it was apparent that no more buses were coming. What this implied only partially sunk in. They continued to search. Believed they saw her face in the crowd. Thought maybe she was among those who had gone into the hotel to get some sleep. They kept on like this. Searched the bathrooms. Made an announcement at the reception desk. Several times, Otto ran over to the supermarket on the other side of the street. Marie may have gone directly over there, she was probably famished. He checked at the gas station too. And there he found a boy who thought he had seen Marie at the campsite when the shooting had begun. He studied the photo carefully as he took large bites of his hamburger. He nodded. That was her, he was almost certain. Sofie came over and looked as though she wanted to tear the food from the poor boy's hands. She bombarded him with questions. No, he didn't know what she was doing at the tent. Getting something, probably. No, he hadn't seen where she'd run to. Yes, he was pretty sure that she ran too, because they heard the shouts and someone screaming that they should escape. The boy had looked at them in anguish, as though he understood that this was all that they would ever know. He backed out through the door.

The night was long, though at the same time much too short. They wandered around in the large

143

hotel garden, where old trees shed gloom onto all that they knew. Sofie still clung to a hope. In the morning, they sat with the others in the spacious dining hall. They ate a completely normal breakfast. Coffee, bread, eggs. Normality was tantalizingly close. Later, the prime minister and the royal family came, and for Otto it felt as though order was restored to the land. But it was different for Sofie. She tore herself away and left. Otto observed that all of the lucky ones clustered together. They went home with their children, were considerate, didn't say farewell to those who were left with vacant gazes, their mobile phones pressed to their chests. Suddenly, there was someone who must have received terrible news, a woman began to sob. The faces of those still waiting, the faces in which the hours had slowly switched off hope, extinguishing it completely. He went to look for Sofie, and found her in the garden.

'I can't be here,' she whispered. 'Help me. Help me, Otto. I can't. I can't.'

He had supported her over to the car and drove her home. The house was so quiet. They sat on Marie's bed, holding hands. Soon they would know everything. Where she had been found. Where the bullets had gone in. The vital organs that had been damaged. The amount of time that had passed before they'd found her. But the hours that they sat in her room, unknowing, among the chaos she had made as she'd packed . . . for this short period it was as though nothing had happened, there was a kind of peace. Then the news came, they were informed, and Sofie began tidying the drawers. She started feverishly in on Marie's bureau, pulling out drawer after drawer, folding her underwear together, her undershirts, T-shirts, sorting the socks and pulling them together in a pair. She was unstoppable, swatting Otto away when he tried to come close, thereafter going to their own closet, sorting the drawer of socks, the drawer of undergarments, everything rapidly, as her tears and nose ran. For a while, Otto shut himself into the washroom in order to escape the sight and sound of her. Again he witnessed something extinguishing in her eyes, that Sofie, that thing which was her inner light, vanished.

The light from the door. Each time Sofie opened her eyes. She had to open them now and then, because this transition to sleep, in which dreams suddenly become thoughts and thoughts become dreams, might lead to places she didn't wish to enter. She had been thinking about the new rainstorm predicted for the weekend, and then her thoughts drifted further to the painting of Karl Johan in the rain, the street like a grey river, black parasols. And yet iridescent, too, there was so much light and strength in this painting. And then came the sentence, spoken innocently to Marie, which always struck Sofie like a lightning bolt: *I hope you never grow up*. Her throat restricted, she had to sit up, try to locate her breath. These are the kinds of ridiculous things that mothers say because they're drowning in love. And Marie had smiled patronizingly. Nothing was going to stop her, not least her mother's wishful thinking. The die had already been cast, she was on her way.

Sofie remained sitting upright in bed for a while. The blackbird had already begun to sing. Which meant that the time must be around five o'clock. Blackbird in the black night. Wasn't Otto coming soon? Sofie lay the blanket over her feet, and propped her head against the wall. Perhaps she could sleep like this for a while.

Otto sat with his feet out in front of him, stretching them and flexing. His dancing feet. He still had quite handsome toes. Sofie said that as well, she liked to massage his feet. Sometimes they sat, each on one end of the sofa, massaging each other's feet. He curled his toes together and spread them out, repeated the actions systematically. Sofie was waiting in there, he could tell. They still had this powerful connection between them, he could nearly always recall the magic from their first meeting. What is more romantic than meeting at a wedding? A summer wedding, dinner indoors, coffee and dancing outdoors in the garden. A colleague of Otto's had wed a woman who worked at the art museum. She'd invited several of her colleagues, a whole flock of gorgeous women waiting, at his disposal. The rumour had preceded him:

Otto was a good dancer. He was one of the few people who really could dance, and who kept at it all evening. His shirt was soaked after the third dance. He noticed Sofie. Surely you can dance tango, he said to her as he met her on the way out of the washroom. Is it so obvious, she smiled. The dance floor was outside beneath the open sky, and it soon began to rain. That was most likely what had done the trick, what had captivated him. That she kept on dancing. She didn't ask questions, didn't stop, didn't complain that her hair, her back, her shoulders got wet. They were concentrated. A warmth between them. The rain closed in on them. There was nothing but them, in a close and increasingly more melancholy dance.

And then the walks between the trees, before the kiss, before they held hands. Dawn light, it stopped raining, all of the wedding guests had gone their separate ways, and here they were. A path looped around a tranquil pond. She had learnt to dance tango in Buenos Aires and told this story about a widower who danced with his deceased wife. Held his arms out in front as though holding a woman, and danced. He came to the milonga, the large dance hall, the same day each week. Always dressed elegantly. A friendly face. Precise steps. Extend a hand, swing around. Sometimes he would venture some words to her. Sometimes it rained through the roof. The tourists went home, but those who belonged kept dancing. Sofie recounted the story, and this also turned into the story about them. Because hadn't Otto thought on this first morning that he and Sofie should become a couple like that, a couple who held one another, steered one another through life, into old age, and hopefully into death? Yes, thought Otto, hopefully into death.

She must have been sleeping a bit, at least nodded off, because there was Otto beside her. Without the blanket, he too, she could see his contours where he lay with his back to her, curled together like a child. It was almost completely dark in the room. She turned and caressed his arm. He grunted weakly. She led her hand along his side, down towards his stomach. Sweat in the creases of his skin. 'What have you been up to?' she whispered. She didn't receive a response. But there was a feeble movement as she passed her hand lightly over his penis. She stroked further down his thigh. It was coated entirely in a thin layer of sweat. Normally when he got clammy it was a sign that he was sick or nervous or didn't feel like it. But now he was warm. She crept towards his back. She was sweaty and he was sweaty. She kept stroking his penis, which had begun to get stiff. The room was pitch dark, she didn't have any idea what time it was. She didn't have any idea what she wanted. It was a kind of restlessness. Her hand stroked, massaged, rubbed. She received no other response than the small, friendly thrusts from his cock. Finally, she sat upright, placed a knee on each side of his hips. He wasn't completely firm, but still slipped in, they were both so slick and wet.

She began moving slowly up and down. Dissociated thoughts and images surfaced in the rhythm that was created. A joke about menopause, that one turned wet outside and dry on the inside. Otto's expression when he nailed shut the veranda door. The image of the storm, enormous, old trees fallen across a road. The limp sails of the model ship. A maelstrom. The thoughts fluttered past, but didn't catch.

She must concentrate. Because he didn't stiffen up inside of her, it rather seemed as though he became limper. She had waited for a response, and there it came. A weak thrust from his hips. And one more. And then his voice, muted, distorted.

'Sofie, I don't really know if . . . '

She worked herself up. Rotated, rubbed. Everything became increasingly featureless, fleeting. Her orgasm was like a string, a wound opening upward from her groin. She gasped. He was completely outside of her. And then she felt his hands around her hips, he helped her off. She crept back to her side of the bed, where the sheet was clammy and creased. She fumbled for her pillow and stuck it between her wet thighs. Otto turned over on his side, she could feel his warm breath against her ear. Wasn't he going to say anything?

She lay waiting for a feeling of shame that didn't come. Instead she felt relaxed, at peace. After a while she could hear from his breath that he was asleep.

MONDAY

Sofie drove quickly, it was late. Otto was desperately trying to get a hold of someone to repair the veranda door. She listened to the many failed telephone conversations with her gaze fixed to the road. She was actually too tired to drive. The little sleep that she'd got had been filled with strange dreams. With only simple images and sensations as remnants. Escape, forest, sharp teeth. But one dream came through clearly, and that was what she called her recurring dream. It continued to return in new variations. The dream was about someone entrusting a child to her. The child was always a girl. She was four or five years old. It was never Marie, none of the girls in these dreams resembled her. The reasons why Sofie was supposed to take the girl were unclear. This was the way of dreams. But the child was there, and the days began to feel ordinary, and the child became her child. They were a family. After these dreams she would awaken with a good and warm feeling. A good feeling of finally having responsibility for a child once again. But today there had been so many other unclear dream images in the way.

When at last Otto gave up and put down his mobile phone, they were on their way into the city. They could glimpse it up ahead, pressed between low hills. They drove along Mossevegen, a green corridor with the fjord gleaming between the trees on one side. On the other lay old wooden houses with gardens like green hollows and new low rises presenting disproportional verandas made of glass and steel. It was going to be a warm day. The traffic moved more and more slowly and finally came to a full stop. Sofie drummed on the steering wheel, Otto looked at the clock. The minutes passed, Sofie rolled down the window on her side. A salty sting in the exhaust-heavy air. The sea shimmered. Otto switched on the radio. There was talk about the flood crisis, now it was mostly about numbers, damages, staggering estimates about how much it would end up costing society. The line of cars shifted a few metres forward, and then it stopped again. They were a part of this sluggish, grey river between all that whirred and shone.

Look at the kind of life we lead, thought Otto. Here we are, enclosing ourselves in little tins, and around us this abundance. This enormous generosity displayed to us, year after year. Which we are unable to accept. Further in, the high rises with glass facades repelled the sunlight strongly back. City life: radiant and dirty. So chaotic. Truly a bitter pleasure. Just think that the city must have also seemed like that to those people who came rattling into town a hundred years ago. Three hundred years ago. A dump, a cesspit. But with illuminated streets and doors to open, many places to enter. Little Oslo. As all cities, with its own rules, as all cities in its own way unhealthy, dangerous. And we want to go in there, thought Otto. Every one of us.

The treetops swayed across the roadway on the side where he sat, wild grass burst from cracks in the ground. A bit of rain, and everything was at it again. The entire machinery. The ocean pierced thin needles of light in through the driver's side window. Sofie leant back in her seat and closed her eyes.

'There must be an accident,' said Otto.

'I think I'll have to go straight to work,' said Sofie.

'Then you should drive me home first, I need to change.'

Sofie cast a glance at him and nodded. She had found a clean jean skirt for herself at the cabin, one that reached down below her knees, together with her blue shirt it would have to do as her work outfit. She couldn't risk coming too late to the kickoff. Karin had sent her a text message that a lot of people had come in over the weekend, especially on Sunday. Good for us, she thought. Good for Wegelmann. The familiar pains began creeping back into her shoulders and hips. It was also sore around her tick bite, although the swelling had gone down a bit in the night. Small strands of pain shot up from her wrist to her elbow. There we have it, she thought. The poison is on its way towards the heart.

'I don't know whether I was able to secure the cabin well enough. There's no one who can take the job until sometime in October.'

'It seemed to me that you did a very solid job.'

The queue began to loosen up. They slugged forward, a few metres at a time. Otto rolled down his window and leant out, trying to get a glimpse of what had occurred up ahead.

'Police and ambulance,' he announced. 'Looks like a collision.'

Soon they came to a policeman directing the cars carefully around the scene of an accident.

'Don't look,' said Otto. He himself stretched out his neck. A delivery truck halfway out of the ditch, in front of a small passenger car with its entire side crunched in. Among the chaos he saw the sparks from a cutting torch.

'You said that *I* shouldn't look,' Sofie said. And then: 'What do you see?'

'They're trying to cut someone out of the wreck.'

Otto said nothing about the limp hand hanging at a strange angle from the glass, or the kid that a policewoman was trying to pull away. But Sofie could hear his wail.

'Does it look serious?'

'Yes.'

It was behind them now, but the mirrors still reflected the pulsating blue lights of the police car. Sofie breathed. In through the nose, out through the mouth.

'You saw it, didn't you?'

'I saw something. But I can't say how hurt she was.'

'So it was a woman?'

He nodded. 'I'm quite sure.'

Her arm had been brown and slender. Was it her head that he had glimpsed through the splintered glass? Or had he imagined it? A bowed neck, a head drooping forward, the hair hanging down, her face hidden.

'How was she sitting? Was she bleeding?'

'Sofie, stop it.'

They continued driving in silence, rode through the new, effective traffic machines. The streets narrowed, buildings of flats rose up, pavements and roadways overflowing with bicyclists, children on scooters, dogs prancing here and there with their gangs. Sofie slowed down, blinkered in to Jens Bjelkes Gata, had to stop for a flock of children. A daycare outing. Each of them with small, green reflective vests, two by two, hand in hand, chattering and exuberant. On their way to the greenhouse, or maybe to the swimming pool. Behind the tiny flock, the street lay like a tunnel of light. Sofie pushed down the visor. Their neighbourhood could appear like two completely different worlds from one day to the next.

She dropped Otto off at the gate, he rummaged through the trunk. It was full of black sacks of rubbish and boxes of things that they had brought back to repair and clean.

'I can't get everything,' he called up to her. 'The damned rug . . . '

'OK, we'll do it this evening.'

Otto waited until Sofie had driven away, stood for a moment with the sensation of being stretched and then wrenched loose. He loaded himself with sacks and bags and hauled himself up to the fifth floor. The air in the flat was heavy, a slight odour of rotten fruit. Otto found a tick as he showered that hadn't been there when he'd checked the previous evening. He could feel the tiny clump as he soaped between his groin. Swearing and dripping wet, he dug through the cupboard to find a pair of tweezers. As he pulled out the tiny fleck of an animal, a few hairs came as well. It stung, he swore again. The damned vermin. It sucked all the joy out of nature. It was impossible to appreciate a meadow or a small forest without simultaneously picturing to himself hundreds of creeping blood-suckers. These invisible pests had slowly but surely invaded the country. According to the latest reports, they could now be found all the way up to the tree line, always bringing with them new types of infections.

Otto had to dry the bathroom after he'd dried himself, he had left wet pools everywhere. When he'd finally pulled on a clean shirt and a light pair of trousers, he saw that there were several unanswered calls on his mobile phone. There was also a text message from Karin. He let off drying his hair, simply tossed his wallet and keys into his bag and hurried down the stairs as he began reading the message. But suddenly the mobile phone hovered in front of him in the air like a silver arrow, and his body felt light and free. When the neighbour opened the door, Otto was lying on his stomach on the outside landing, with his feet upon the lowest step. He had passed out for a moment.

'Are you hurt?' the neighbour asked nervously. 'Are you hurt?'

Hurt was a word that had little to do with the surreal, pounding feeling, the burning, the nausea, the fluttering. Otto couldn't discern where the various sensations originated, or where they were going. He could feel that it hurt to lift his head, so he lay it back down. If he could only keep from moving, it would all be OK, he thought, before everything went black again. The next thing he knew, he was lying on his back, and a man was shining a light into his eyes with a small torch.

'What is your name?' asked the man with the torch.

'Otto,' said Otto. He could hear that his voice was unsteady, felt something warm dribbling down his chin.

'Do you know what day it is today?'

Otto tried looking around him, but it was difficult to turn his head. He had been given some kind of collar. The only thing he could see was the blue-grey walls of the stairway, and the long, concerned face of his neighbour who stood holding onto the banister. He was wearing a short brown dressing gown. From his position on the floor, Otto was able to see too much of his pale, hairy thighs. They rarely saw this neighbour, but they often noticed the cigarette smoke that percolated out from his flat. Sofie was convinced that he sat indoors day and night watching TV and smoking. Now Otto would be able to inform her that the man sat watching TV and smoking in nothing but his dressing gown.

'Monday,' mumbled Otto.

'Good, you're with us. You've taken a bad fall, but now we are going to bring you to the emergency room to examine you properly.'

The man with the torch signalled, and a young man with curls hanging down to his eyes came into Otto's periphery. He looked just like Peter. 'Oh, hi,' Otto mumbled, surprised. And then there was lifting and easing. The rug, even with straps. There was nothing to do but let it happen. Otto tried uttering thanks as they bore him past the neighbour, but found it difficult to move his lips.

After the kickoff meeting, Sofie grabbed a coffee with Aasmund and Frank, another of the curators. She had received several compliments on her simple attire, people said she looked particularly summery. Could it really bother anyone that she tended to wear black? And could it make them happy when she stopped? She sat on the edge of the conference table, dangling her feet, feeling like a young girl in a film from the fifties. Summery, summer-light, carefree. She made the men laugh. Told about the frog beneath the lampshade and how she and Otto had fought about the unlocked door. She received a call from reception. There was a Hopstock waiting who wished to speak with her. Perplexed, she said that he should wait there, and she would be downstairs soon.

'Oh, no . . . ' she said as soon as the announcement had been made.

'What? Bad news?'

Aasmund sat there so confidently, arms spread behind his neck, feet up on the table. What was it about men who spread out like that? Was it a need to mark their territory, or had they simply always been at liberty to take up so much space? Sofie stood.

'No, I just don't want to meet him.'

'Why didn't you say that you weren't available?'

'Yes, why didn't I say that I wasn't available? Imagine if there was an answer to that.'

Aasmund waved gleefully as she left. Sofie swore into the stairwell wall as she descended. Steeled herself. What in the world did this man want? She noticed him at once, he stood staring vacantly into a showcase. Tall and stooped, his wavy hair, a worn leather bag across his shoulder. He looked troubled, his lips were pale. He spotted her too, stood ready with hand outstretched and a lopsided smile as she came over to him.

'Hi Sofie. Thank you for taking the time. It's probably very busy here right now.'

'Yes, it is.'

She could hear herself that it was short and deprecatory.

'I came to ask your pardon,' he said quickly. 'It won't take very long, I promise.'

They couldn't continue standing there. A group of Spanish tourists were talking vociferously among themselves and with the coatroom attendant. Sofie hesitated, and then led him with a wave over to the tiny coffee bar. It was nearly empty so early in the day. She found a table right next to the door and signalled to Eveyln behind the counter to bring coffee.

'Thank you,' he said and hung his bag on the chair. Sofie gestured for him to be seated, and then sat down too, on the edge of her chair.

'I don't want to keep you long,' he said folding his hands in front of him on the table. 'I just needed to, as I mentioned, beg your pardon for my behaviour on Saturday.'

Sofie was glad that Evelyn arrived at that moment with the coffee, for it allowed her not to respond immediately. Why did he come to her? He couldn't have decided to look up each and every one of the guests and go around asking forgiveness for his behaviour, could he? Lasse Hopstock pushed at the cup and continued:

'I'm not referring to the pathetic performance that I gave after dinner, even though I should probably beg pardon for that as well. But I was completely indelicate when I went on heckling you about sorrows and secrets . . . Now I know what you've been through. Yes, there was talk about you after you'd both left. I, of anyone, should know better than to trample over peoples' boundaries in that way. It was therefore important for me to come here and ask your pardon. I am truly sorry that I was so intrusive.'

Sofie opened her mouth and shut it again. She was going to say that it was all right, but it hadn't been all right at all. And now she began to picture these people sitting there with their half-full glasses and their empathetic expressions, discussing her. That didn't feel all right either.

'I know that an apology isn't enough, you probably won't accept it, but I just wanted to say it anyway. Many people who lost children in the same . . . tragedy . . . have been my clients. So I know something about what you've been through. And for that reason, I feel even more ashamed than I have for many years. I often behave like an idiot, but to engage in that type of mental bullying as I did, it was indelicate and thoughtless of me.'

Sofie was unable to look at him while he spoke. She looked down at the table, she looked at her hands, and then her gaze fixed somewhere to the right of his face before gliding out through the glass doors. The Spanish tourists were no longer in sight, but Karin rushed in, past the reception with a shopping bag, and cast a long glance in at them.

'You don't have to say anything. I probably shouldn't have imposed myself on you again, but I wanted to say that I can understand very well that you are angry. And there's one more thing that I wish to say, and it's a bit more difficult.'

He pushed the saucer of the tiny white cup back and forth, but calmly. He still hadn't taken a sip of coffee.

'I should be careful not to say that know anything about you whatsoever, Sofie. But what I do know, is that my clients, who have experienced something similar to you, have had a great many traumas and emotions to deal with. I'm not saying that talking to a professional is helpful for everyone, and certainly not all the time, but in particular circumstances it can be a kind of safeguard.'

'Safeguard?'

She said it flatly. He pushed his glasses upward, their eyes met.

'Safeguard. There are many other words I could use. But I believe you understand what I mean.'

He retrieved a card from his pocket. White with black typeface and a red symbol that looked like a vine.

'Here is my card, and the name of my colleague here in the city is written on the back. Both she and

I would be able to make time for you immediately. So, now I am not going to bother you any longer.'

As he said farewell, he held her hand a few seconds too long. Sofie was confused. She was angry, but she also felt completely calm. He had gone too far. Again. But there was a genuine earnestness that emanated from him.

'Thank you for listening to me, Sofie. I wish you all the best.'

The escalator carried her up, away from him, lifted her away from this encounter which had been something more than just unpleasant. In a strange way, it had also smoothed something out, put her in a calm state. And perhaps created an opening, but for what? She let the stairs bear her upwards through the museum. Only when she was back in her office did she look down at her phone. Someone had called several times. She didn't know the number, and the voice on the machine was also unfamiliar:

'Hi, this is from the officer on duty at the Emergency Room. We have brought in your husband after a fall on the stairs. He is being examined right now, you may call this number.'

Her knees began to tremble, she couldn't control them, had to sit down. Karin, who had just walked past in the corridor, backed up and stuck her head in.

'Sofie, has something happened?'

She came in and shut the door behind her.

'What is it? You're white as a ghost.'

'I just got a call from the ER. Otto fell down the stairs.'

'My God . . . But how serious is it?'

'No idea. I can't bring myself to call.'

'Would you like me to do it?'

Sofie looked for a long while at her mobile phone, and then looked at Karin with the same empty gaze.

'No, I have to talk to them myself.'

She picked up the phone. Karin pulled back.

'I'll wait outside.'

A man picked up. Sofie didn't know how to form the words, but he understood her point immediately.

'Him, yes, he came in with the ambulance a while ago.'

'The ambulance?' Sofie almost whispered.

'Yes, he was pretty beat up,' the man said lightly. 'But he's OK now, I mean,' he added quickly. 'I believe,' he concluded, mumbling, as though he may not be too sure after all.

'But what . . . ' her voice wavered completely.

'They are examining him right now. He is totally conscious, I can ask him to call you when they're done with the examination.'

'I'm on my way now,' said Sofie.

Queen Eufemias Gata stretched out before her in the sweltering sun, nearly deserted. The city's latest promenade was actually a bridge, resting on eleven hundred stilts above the old sea floor. The street had sunk several centimetres in only a few years, as had most of the high rises in Bjørvika. Muddy, muddy, Sofie chanted internally as she half-sprinted, half-walked along the wide walkway. She needed a word, a rhythm to keep the worst images at bay. A crushed skull, a cracked collarbone, teeth knocked out . . . her fantasy had free reign. In between, the face of Lasse Hopstock surfaced, his fixed gaze behind those whacky round spectacles. That calm, monotonous voice of his. Muddy, muddy. Halfway down the street it dawned on her that she'd forgotten the car. At first she continued on, but soon realized that she would need the car to transport Otto back home. She turned and walked rapidly back. The street was wide and long and strangely sterile, despite that much work had been put into giving it a touch of greenery. The columnar English oaks that had been planted along the tram line had begun to wane. There had been several discussions about what might be ailing the trees. Some believed the dead trees should be replaced with fresh ones, others thought it better to give up the entire row. There's always someone who just wants to tear everything out. Muddy, muddy. The soles of her feet burnt. Sofie ran the last few metres towards the parking garage.

At the Emergency Room, she was asked to go sit in the waiting room until Otto was finished.

'They are stitching him up now. We'll let them know you're here.'

She found a bench by the window. A young woman was waiting there too, thin, light hair and painfully tight jeans. From where she sat, bent with eyes shut, it wasn't possible to see whether she was in pain, was drugged up or was merely shutting out the world. At the other end of the waiting room, a woman murmured quietly in a language Sofie couldn't understand. Her complaints escalated each time a nurse walked through the room. Sofie recalled having been here once before, with a friend of Marie's who had been spending the night. What was her name again? Couldn't she remember the names of her daughter's friends any longer? In any case, she had cut her hand when the girls were helping to make Friday tacos. What an uproar it had been. Waiting among the chaos here on a Friday night, with sick and drugged people staggering about, with two small girls, one hand wrapped in paper towels, and trying, over the phone, to calm her parents, who were at their mountain cabin. It had been so long ago, this life with so much to organize, little girls going out and in, calling here and there.

Sofie looked around. Pale-coloured walls, the benches were no longer plastic. On the wall above the woman who sat complaining was a poster with an enormous picture of a tick. It was some kind of warning poster. Sofie thought, in any case, it must have been created to scare immigrants from taking their children out into the forests and meadows. The greatly enlarged tick looked more dangerous than any bear or moose, those animals that one had been taught to watch out for in her childhood. She went over to read what was written there. There was a small list of illnesses borne by ticks, with a list of symptoms. Sofie noticed that she stood rubbing the bracelet she had put on to hide her tick bite. It stung a bit. She identified with too many of these symptoms. But that's always how it is, she thought. If you read about illness, you suddenly start believing that everything's the matter with you.

A half hour passed before someone came to get her. A woman in a white coat. Are you the next of kin for Otto Krohg-Iversen? Kinsfolk. Survivor. Are there any language researchers who have analysed these types of terms? Sofie wondered, following the white-clad woman. Betrothed. Forbear. There were many words like that. Offspring. Not all of them sounded as good.

He was sitting at the end of the corridor. Without many recognizable features left on his swollen face, which was covered with bloody lacerations, bruises and bandages. Sofie didn't say a word, only offered him an arm. On the way out, Otto spoke slowly and unclearly, attempting to trivialize the entire ordeal and complaining that his mobile phone had been smashed in the fall. It was difficult for him to get into the car, so she had to recline the passenger seat flat backwards. Then he confessed that the doctor had found a few cracked ribs as well. And in addition, they suspected that he had suffered a concussion, so he had been given one week's leave from work and a supply of strong painkillers. A note from the doctor stated that he would have to be woken up hourly on the first day, to be certain there wasn't any bleeding in the brain.

'Oh my God, Otto.'

'It's only just in case.'

It was hard for him to ascend the stairs, and once he entered the flat, he toppled over onto the sofa and was asleep almost immediately. Sofie tip-toed softly around, didn't quite know what to do. He hadn't even changed his clothes, there was blood on his shirt, and his light grey trousers were dirty and blotched. She unbuttoned some of the buttons, loosened up his clothes, sat and looked at him. He breathed heavily through his mouth. His nose was red and bruised, solidified blood was caked around his nostrils. Sofie realized that she should probably tell some people. Peter had his own worries, and anyway it was late where he was, but shouldn't he nonetheless be informed? In the end, Sofie sent him a brief text message that his father had fallen down the stairs and been badly beat up, but that it didn't seem to be serious. Peter called immediately.

'Hi, is it you,' said Sofie gladly. 'It's so nice that you're calling!'

She walked into the library and pulled the sliding door shut. And then she explained to Peter what had happened. He seemed shaken up.

'I'm not used to something being wrong with *my old man*,' he said.

'No, he's never sick. I've also been struggling with the situation,' said Sofie.

There was silence between them for a moment. A quiet handshake.

'But how are things going with you?' asked Sofie.

'I've been at the hospital getting a few tests.'

'What kind of tests?'

'Ultrasound and the like. There was something in my blood tests that wasn't right. But they can't find anything.'

Peter spoke quickly, as though trying to run from his own words.

'Does your father know about this?'

'He doesn't know about the tests. Would you tell him?'

'Oh, Peter.'

'I'm doing fine. Go look out for my dad now.'

Narrow strips of light from the almost-closed blinds fell across Otto. Sofie looked at the clock. Perhaps she should wake him up more often than every other hour, at least in the beginning. But as she sat on the edge of the sofa and lay her hands carefully on his chest, his eyes flew open. His gaze narrowed.

'It doesn't help anything to look at me like that!'

She retracted her hands. Otto shut his eyes again, to keep from seeing her. The rage that surged up in Sofie was so unexpected, so powerful that it felt as though strong hands had grabbed hold of her and yanked her up onto her legs. Something as clumsy and unnecessary as falling down the stairs. She stared down at his face. God only knew whether he would ever become his old self again. Scuffed up skin, lips blue and grotesque. Sofie pictured herself striking this face with her clenched fists, smashing her fists down into his minced-meat kisser, once, twice . . .

She took a few stiff steps towards the kitchen. We've been through worse things, she thought. We've been through worse.

Otto complained of a headache each time Sofie woke him. She read the doctor's note once more and gave him as many painkillers as had been prescribed. He lay in a daze, it wasn't easy extracting anything sensible from him. How in the world should she know whether his brain was bleeding? But at some point into the evening he seemed to revive. He asked her to find a newscast, which he listened to with his eyes shut. It was an update on the clean-up work, and forecasts about which areas the coming storm would hit hardest. There was a report from Denmark, that they were trying to contain a large oil spill after a tanker had been driven ashore. And there was a new boat disaster with refugees in the Mediterranean. It went on and on. Otto inhaled deeply.

'And I'm supposed to sit here and listen to these discouraging news stories—for how many days? No reading, no watching television, scarcely any thinking.'

'There's more than just news on the radio, you know. I'm taking the day off tomorrow to stay at home with you.'

'There's no reason to do that. But you do have my permission to buy me a new mobile phone.'

'So the old one is totally destroyed?'

'Completely wasted. But I was able to take out the SIM card.'

'I'll go get some audio books too. You've always said you don't have time to read. Now's your chance.'

Karin called to ask how things were going. Sofie hinted that perhaps Otto wasn't in the best of moods, and described how he looked. Frankenstein of Tøyen. Karin laughed.

'It's no joke having a sick man at home,' she said. 'Can we both go out tomorrow after work, get a glass of wine? There's something I would like to speak with you about.'

Sofie hesitated, said that she didn't want to leave Otto lying there like that.

'Maybe later in the week,' she said.

'It's just that . . . I saw you talking to a certain man in the cafe today.'

'A certain man? Oh, yes, I noticed that you walked past.'

'You see, I know him. And there's something I have to tell you . . . But it's not something to discuss on the phone. I actually think it's essential we have a glass of wine when we talk about him. Maybe an entire bottle.'

'Now I'm starting to get really curious.'

'You should be. Five o'clock tomorrow? At Palmen?'

Otto looked at her queerly when she said she would be going out with Karin the following day.

'I don't understand. Are you suddenly friends again now?'

'It's clear that you don't understand. Karin and I have never been enemies.'

Otto had pulled himself half up on the sofa. Sofie got a few extra pillows and propped them behind his back. The blood had soaked through one of the bandages on his forehead.

'But if you feel insecure about Karin, maybe it's better to keep your distance?'

'First you say it's silly of me to have a falling out with Karin, and now you're advising me to keep my distance?'

Something creaked. The sound came from inside his head. Otto identified it as fear. It grew. It might loosen, fall.

'No, I didn't mean it like that. You should absolutely go out. Sitting here watching me heal is worse than sitting and watching paint dry. After all, paint doesn't go and snap at you in spite of everything.'

She smiled. He patted her on the hands.

'You should have more friends than Karin. That's what I meant. You almost never go out. Not with friends, not just to chat and have a good time. You don't have friends any more.'

175

'But we have a lot of friends. More than we can gather together around our table.'

'Those are our common friends, our social circle. But how many girlfriends do you actually have, girlfriends to whom you can disclose everything?'

'How many friends like that do you have?' parried Sofie.

They stared at one another, ready for the fight, spring-loaded. Otto's patched-up face broke into a grin.

'Listen to us,' he said.

'You still haven't answered my question.'

'And you haven't answered mine. Sofie, just accept it. We no longer have any close friends. And it's our own faults. We pull back, withhold from people until they give up. You need someone to talk with, to relax with, someone other than me.'

'I have Judit.'

'Yes. Your sister. And when was the last time you spoke to her?'

'What does that have to do with it?'

'So, your sister is your closest friend. But you don't talk to her much either. Could it be that you *aren't* in fact such good friends at the moment?'

Sofie merely glared at him.

'It's about the photos, Sofie. I have to say that I can understand her somewhat.'

'It's not true, what she says. I've never forbidden her to hang up photos of Marie.'

'You had the same controversy with your mother, that's the reason why you don't have much contact with her either. Or am I wrong?'

Sofie's mouth was a narrow line. Otto tried sitting all the way up, but fell back on the pillows with a moan.

'I should probably be careful about what I say. It looks like I'm going to be dependent on your goodwill for a while.'

'I've never forbidden anyone to display photos of Marie, you know that. It's when they begin to build these small altars at home . . . with flowers and angels and plastic hearts and God knows what . . . and when it comes to my mother, we only discussed this one photo that she'd had enlarged, and it wasn't enough that it was blurry, she looked completely . . . '

Sofie threw her arms helplessly into the air.

'No, it wasn't the best photo of her. Because you're the one who has the best photos of Marie, and you aren't going to give them to anyone.'

The sun had set, tones of blue pressed their way into the room, August evenings can have a deep hue. Sofie turned on the kitchen light and began whisking eggs into an omelette. She wanted to whisk air and love into the omelette for her injured husband, but suspected that it contained more despondency and frustration than anything. She thought of her father. You're a daddy's girl, Otto would tell her. Maybe he was right. Her father was the only one who had supported her—or, at least, had a kind of understanding—in the controversies that she'd waged with her sisters and mother, everyone else stayed well enough away. But when Sofie thought of her parents, she thought of them as a single being. Gustav and Else Krohg had always worked together, travelled together, been together on everything. Together they had run the tiny publishing house. Her father read aloud to her from French and American literary magazines at the breakfast table and, for his daughters' bedtime stories, excerpts from manuscripts he favoured. They often had guests for dinner, Judit and Sofie would find out from newspaper interviews that they were well-known authors. As adults, they couldn't distinguish memories of one face from the other, only the constant din of voices and people patting their heads, remarking in English that they had such nice dresses, such nice hair.

Sofie had foreseen that she would take over the publishing company one day, and her father had too, but then she went to Vienna and got married and had a child, and Judit began her medical studies. When her mother and father retired, they sold the publishing house without much discussion. They had seen how difficult that line of work was going to become.

Otto ate a few mouthfuls of the omelette. It was obvious it hurt him to chew. His bottom lip was swollen and he had sores inside his mouth. She should have made soup. He mumbled something about more painkillers. She took his plate and asked whether he wouldn't like to undress, to go to bed. There was no response. Sofie curled up on the other sofa, but sleep eluded her. Her one arm felt strange, like an animal that had bitten her shoulder and was now just hanging on. As she lay there, she felt a kind of relief that Otto had obviously forgotten about the bite. But the pain was constant. She was going to tell him that when she got the chance. The pain is constant.

Was it possible for anyone else to understand what it meant that Marie hadn't called? That everything had been completely silent from her side that evening, even though they'd found her mobile phone next to her, with all of those unanswered calls. Why hadn't Marie called her mother? Had she not had time? Or did she not dare, out of fear of moving, making a noise? Or had she known, as she crept behind that boulder—and that was almost the worst thought—that there was no one who could help her?

The questions had surfaced later at gatherings, among those few surviving relatives who had been able to meet with one another, and they had been tossing around within her ever since. The parents talked about those last desperate conversations. There was a dad who had only heard his daughter's screams. There was a mother who'd had enough time to say how much she loved her son. Most of the kids had called their parents, their friends. From their hiding places behind trees and boulders and beneath rocky outcroppings, they had sent text messages, tweeted or called. They had sobbed, despaired, informed, received advice, said goodbye. The worst imaginable phone conversation in the world, but it was unbearable not to have it.

Had she fallen asleep, after all? Sofie opened her eyes, and directly before her was a towering figure. So, there he was again, gallingly close. How could she know what it was that she saw? There was no visible face, no feet, no hands, she was merely staring into those black trousers. They were of a stiff, hard fabric, and she could see a belt, the gleam of a buckle. It was as though a lightning bolt flashed, a reflector illuminated, and then he was gone. Sofie sat up on the sofa. Her heart was pounding, she could feel the pulse down along her aching arm. Just come, she wanted to scream. Just come, show yourself, show your face, you most cowardly of all cowards. Just come, with your fake uniform, your bleached fringe, those whitened teeth of yours, those big ideas that you have about yourself. You most wretched of all wretches, you who shoots children from behind.

The room had become dim. From the street, muffled sounds, the distinct smell of rain. Slowly, Sofie was able to urge time and the room back into place. She must wake Otto and convince him to go lay down in the bed. Two dirty plates lay between them on the table. In that very space and moment, it all seemed like much too much to set in motion. The body on the sofa, limp and powerless, the plates on the table, one of them with leftover bits of omelette.

Marie hadn't been one of the first that he'd found as he began his jaunt around the island. She had most likely run around for a while, trying out various hiding places. Several people tried down near the water, but after a while every possible hiding place had been taken. Perhaps she had been looking for her two friends. But they were in the school building, there were thirteen who lay there. Thirteen who fell when he came in and started shooting around. Marie must have been at the washroom, or maybe she'd gone to her tent to get something. She had avoided the first massacre. She'd had a chance. Couldn't she simply have squeezed in somewhere? Couldn't she just have begun swimming? Sofie had created several escape routes for her daughter. In her thoughts, she'd darted down every path, slid down every slope, crept into every cranny. She knew the island in and out now, knew where they had all been hiding, those who survived. She knew the route he had taken, where he had been on the island during each of the seventy-three minutes that his death-lark had lasted.

He found her in the forest, behind a boulder. Two shots through her neck, both fatal. From behind. It could mean that she hadn't seen him. Didn't want to see him. It could mean that his muddy field boots, the swaggering police uniform, that repugnant, cunning, triumphant gaze of his hadn't been the last thing she'd seen of the world. Had she pressed herself into the ground? Had she squeezed her eyes shut, hoped for the best? Played dead, since that was the thing to do when you met a wild animal, such as a bear? But this was not a bear. Perhaps she'd turned her head away, looked at the heather, common heather, the last thing she'd seen, those tiny, dry purple flowers. She hadn't believed in God. Then who had she prayed to? With whom had she spoken in her thoughts?

Her phone was in her rain jacket pocket. There were still batteries. She'd had enough time. And yet she hadn't called anyone.

TUESDAY

She had to pass the government quarter to get to the Human Rights House Foundation. For a long time she had taken large detours to avoid this quarter. And now, regardless, it was nothing but an inaccessible construction zone, gutted of everything except symbolism. The high-rise was still standing. It was impossible to demolish, impossible to use. A concrete skeleton encased in a white sheet, covered by a shroud. An unrequested monument. They hadn't managed to agree on anything in all of these years. That big 'we', the Norwegian people, who had been so unified in the weeks following the tragedy, and who afterwards hadn't been able to reach agreement on a single matter. The buildings wouldn't allow themselves to be filled. The crime scenes wouldn't let themselves be utilized. The memorial would not let itself be erected. Artists who attempted to deal with the national trauma were hushed. The only thing that people wanted to or were able to see, were roses, stars, angels. It was like taping a Hello Kitty plaster over a gaping wound.

Stagnation, thought Sofie as she cycled past and gazed up at the high rise. Status quo. It no longer hurt to look at it. She didn't feel a thing, only a warm breeze, pregnant with the promise of rain. Perhaps stagnation is the only natural response to such a paralysing event? Perhaps it's wrong to desire anything else, thought Sofie, swinging into the street where the Human Rights House Foundation occupied an entire small city blockhouse.

Sofie hadn't been there since the moving-in party in June. It seemed empty and still, though it was early in the day. Were they all travelling? She walked slowly up the stairs, out of breath. Outside, the air was becoming increasingly oppressive and muggy. On each floor, signs declared the names of the organizations that were housed there. The Norwegian Helsinki Committee, Norwegian PEN, the Norwegian Tibet Committee, the Norwegian Organization for Asylum Seekers . . . And at the very top, on the cramped attic level, the Association for the Romani People. So many dedicated individuals, thought Sofie. So many good intentions, and still the world appears the way it does. Just then she registered that someone else was there, a shadow highest up on the stairwell. A woman, her dress fanned out around her. As Sofie came closer, she saw that she was hunched over a small child. The woman looked at her, expressionless, perhaps surprised that she wasn't Otto. What do I do now, thought Sofie. She set down her purse and said hi.

'I am Otto's wife,' she said. The woman reacted to his name. Sofie lifted her hand with the wedding ring, pointed at the ring.

'Wife,' she said.

The child turned in the woman's lap. A small heart-shaped mouth appeared, the eyes were still hidden beneath the scarf. It was not a baby, as Sofie had first thought.

'Girl?' asked Sofie. 'Girl?'

The woman seemed completely apathetic. She must be so hot, thought Sofie. It looked as though she was wearing several skirts layered on top of each other and something that looked like a wool jacket beneath her scarf. Maybe she didn't own anything besides what she wore.

'Can I help you? Do you need help?'

The woman looked up at the door that led into the attic office where Otto's office was. The door was closed.

'Otto won't come today.' Sofie shook her head and made a sad expression. 'Otto has had an accident. He is sick. He's been released from work. Do you understand? Do you understand me?'

The woman turned her eyes downward. Was that a yes?

Sofie sat down on the stairs. Together, the two women stared at the sleeping child. A deep sigh came from the woman, but she still didn't say a word. The tiny girl seemed quite thin. Sofie tried to think. Otto would know what to do, but there was no way to get a hold of him. She could give the woman money, but she didn't have any on her. It didn't seem as though there was anyone in the other offices either. She half-heartedly tried the

187

door on the floor below. Locked. Will she get food? thought Sofie. Will the child get any food? She walked back up the stairs, squeezed past the woman and unlocked the door into Otto's office. The woman began to stand up, but Sofie stopped her with a gesture.

'Wait a minute. Wait. I just want to get something.'

She had been in Otto's office a few times before. It was a minuscule room with a sloped ceiling. The only daylight issued from two skylights, and now the sky outside was turning dark. Sofie switched on the light. She would find what she had come for on the desk, Otto had told her. A portable PC and two red plastic folders which together weighed more than the PC. But there was more there. She stopped with a jolt. Sitting on the desk was a framed photo of Marie and Otto. It had been a long time since she'd seen that photo. She remembered it, but couldn't recall that Otto used to have it on his desk. The photo had been taken by Sofie, it was from Tivoli in Copenhagen, right after Marie and Otto had gone on the Mountain-and-Valley roller coaster. They were smiling and acting dizzy. Marie's dimple was a laser beam through the glass.

Sofie lifted up the picture and studied the frame. Otto must have framed it himself, this photo had never been hanging at home. She quickly pressed her lips to her cheek, to her dimple, the glass. Didn't return the photo to where it had been, but lay it on the desk. So that Otto would know she had seen it.

Two one-hundred crown bills and some small change were in one of the drawers. Relieved, Sofie snatched the bills, stuffed them in her pocket and took the folders and PC out of the office. The woman turned when she came down the stairs. Sofie smiled apologetically as she tried to stuff everything into her bicycle bag. It was already nearly full, with audio books and a box with the new mobile phone.

'I had to get this for Otto, so that he could work a bit from home while he's out on sick leave,' she said, no longer worrying whether the woman understood what she said. When she'd finished snapping the bag shut, she stuck her hand down into her pocket and took out the two one-hundred crown bills.

'And I found these as well. You can buy some food for yourself and your child.'

Sofie stood with the money stretched out towards the woman, who didn't look as though she wanted to take it. Then, suddenly, one of her hands shot out and grasped the hand with the money. Her grip was hard, Sofie had to bend over even further, it was impossible to continue standing like that. She finally had to sit at a squat. The woman turned and twisted her hand. It hurt. Help, thought Sofie. Is she planning to read my fortune? She dropped the money into the woman's lap and opened the palm of her hand upward. However, Sofie soon realized that the woman was staring at the tick bite on her wrist and not at her palm.

'Kerja,' said the woman. She repeated the word, and now she finally looked straight into Sofie's eyes. She wasn't old, she had only seemed so antiquated with her enormous scarf. Sofie could now see that she had some kind of mark along the entire side of her face. It might be a bruise, perhaps from a blow. It might also be a birthmark, but Sofie could feel how hard her heart was pounding in her body. And she, who had tried offering the woman money.

The woman repeated the same word several times, and then uttered several sentences that were just as incomprehensible to Sofie, mixed with one word she understood: *doctor*. The woman stared intensely at her, and Sofie nodded, tried to twist her hand free of the grip.

'Yes. Doctor. Should we go to the doctor?'

She pointed first at the woman, and then at herself. The woman shook her head and pointed decisively at Sofie.

'Doctor.'

Sofie nodded again.

'Come,' she said, standing. 'Come, and we can go to the doctor.'

She grabbed her bicycle bag and held out her other hand towards the woman.

'Come,' she said again, and gestured with a nod, down the stairs, out towards the street. The woman didn't move. She was hunched over the child again, rocking it.

'No?' said Sofie. 'You don't want to come? Not to the doctor?'

The woman didn't look up. Sofie sighed and sat down again on the stairs, one step below the woman. She leant her head back on the wall, perplexed. She needed to return to Otto soon, how was she going to solve this dilemma? One of the paper bills had fallen down onto the step where she sat, the other was crumpled beneath the foot of the sleeping child. Was it normal for a child to sleep so heavily, to sleep like that, in a warm lap, was it even breathing? For one moment, Sofie wondered whether she should take them home with her, the woman and child, tell them that they would go home to Otto, the woman would come in that case, wouldn't she? But she knew that she would have to do better than this. She picked up her phone, looked up a crisis-centre number. The woman who answered said that they could come to the day centre and have a chat with someone there. Sofie noted the address. It wasn't very far away.

'Should I take you, you and your child, somewhere where you can get some help? Should I go with you to the crisis centre? Do you know what that is? Crisis centre. There are only women there, women and other children. You can rest, get food. I can bring you there. If you just come. Come?'

The woman stopped rocking, gathered her hands beneath the child and lifted it up. Lifted it forward, held it raised towards Sofie, with a supplicating but also with a strangely determined expression. The head dangled, the feet dangled. So much hair on such a small child. Sofie didn't know what to do. The child hung in the air in front of her. Her arms longed to take it. She could at least hold the tiny girl for a moment? But it felt like an impossibility to reach out her arms, as though there were a boundary that must not be crossed.

'Plees,' said the woman. 'To diro. Plees. No life.'

So you speak English, thought Sofie weakly. Her resolve had exhausted her through and through. This was starting to resemble her recurring dreams. Someone was holding out a child to her. Should she take it, as she did in the dream?

'No life,' said the woman once more. 'To diro. You life.'

'Yes. And you have life. You have the child.'

Sofie stood to get out of the unnatural position. A woman who refuses to take and hold a child. She stroked the child's stomach, could feel the warmth from the tiny body. The girl was wearing a small, unwashed shirt with a cartoon character on it. Sofie couldn't remember the name of the character, even though Marie and her friends had all had shirts and dresses and pencil cases and bags with the same figure on them. There were always these kinds of figures that small girls wanted on everything.

The child woke now, sniffed, tried to lift its head. The woman pulled her towards herself, put her into her lap. Two dark, hazel eyes met Sofie's clear blue ones.

'Hello, little one,' said Sofie, and tried to blink away her tears. 'Did you have a nice little nap?'

The girl looked at her sceptically, and then twisted towards her mother, buried her face into her breasts.

'Please let me help you,' Sofie asked. 'We'll find a place for you.'

The woman stood as she held the whimpering child tightly to her body with one hand. With the other, she wrapped the scarf around herself and picked up a plastic bag that had been behind her back. Sofie could see a water bottle and some cloth inside the bag. The woman walked stiffly, it was difficult to say whether it was because she was carrying the child, or whether she was hurt somewhere. At the exit, she stopped. Sofie opened the door for them.

It must have rained, a brief shower, there was a scorched aroma. Asphalt, dust. In the days following the storm, the sun had turned blazingly hot in the city. The woman began walking down the street, but in the wrong direction. It wasn't clear whether she had understood what Sofie had told her. She hurried after the woman, the heavy bicycle bag bumping her legs, scraping the skin. She took the woman's arm cautiously, tried to make her turn.

But the woman avoided looking at her and continued to walk, with shuffling steps.

Who had turned a back on whom? Sofie set down her bicycle bag and stood watching the woman and child. Perplexed, aching arms, aching emptiness. The woman's broad back diminished, disappeared down the walkway, across the street and further into a small park. For a while, she could still glimpse them beneath a tree.

'So, in your opinion there isn't anything I could have done differently?'

Sofie had been dreading telling Otto about the meeting outside his office. She knew herself that she had handled the situation badly. He was unwrapping his new mobile phone. She related the story as she stood watching him coax the SIM card into place. It seemed that he hadn't heard what she'd said. Impatiently, she swept the packaging onto the floor. He groaned loudly and tried pulling his legs up as she threw herself down onto the sofa next to him.

'Careful!'

'Explain this to me,' she said, more pleadingly than angry. 'Should I have let her into the office and allowed her to be inside? Or should I have brought her home? Should I have called the police? This is your job. Is it that you don't *want* to answer, or that you *can't*?'

She looked at his eyes, the pain in them, and immediately regretted her outburst.

'To be completely honest, there's not much that you could have done. As long as you don't speak the language . . . If you had been able to get her to the crisis centre, they would probably have sheltered her for a few days, but after that . . . '

'But what would *you* have done?'

He shrugged. 'Spoken to her. Maybe she needed help to fill out a form, find a place to live, I don't know.'

'Kerja,' said Sofie.

'What?'

'That was something she said, several times. "Kerja." Do you know what that means?'

'It depends on how it's used.'

'Just like that. Kerja.'

'It can mean dangerous, painful.'

'She said it about my bite,' said Sofie. 'My insect sting,' she corrected herself.

'Weren't you going to see the doctor about that? Haven't you done that yet? She's absolutely right, it can be dangerous!'

'I've made an appointment. At my regular doctor.'

'When?'

'On . . . ' Sofie thought about it. 'Friday. She didn't have time until Friday.'

'You can't wait until then. I've told you, go to the Urgent Care clinic instead.'

Sofie bent down for the instruction manual, which had landed on the floor together with the packaging. She lay the small booklet on his stomach.

'I don't understand how you're able to do your job. That you don't give up.'

'It's not as hopeless as it appears.'

'No, you have a tendency to say that.'

'These people bear the heaviest burden of anything that happens in Europe. Now they are looking for a way out. Even if they live a lousy life here . . . for some of them, it's a step up.'

Otto watched her vanish up, come down again. She had put on a dress that was almost obscenely short. As compensation, it had long sleeves. Her hair was glossy, she'd put a sharp blue colour on her eyelids. She was beautiful, and he told her. Couldn't she just stay home and sashay around merely for his pleasure? Otto had to admit to himself that he was nervous. It was odd that Karin wanted to meet with Sofie at this particular moment. Might she be considering revealing something? About their text messages? Or about that other thing. Was she threatening to fabricate things? The wording of her last text message to him stuck fresh in his mind. The message that he had just managed to read before losing his footing on the stairs. Perhaps he hadn't read it completely, but something at least had burnt itself into his memory: *You were the one who started it. You took my hand in the taxi. You yourself have said that it means something. Do you think that it will just go away? That it's something we can merely command, like a dog?*

I lack courage, thought Sofie. She was late in leaving. The bus was driving in towards the centre as well as, it seemed, into the rain. She thought about Karin, who was waiting, about what moves she sat contriving. White queen versus black queen? I lack confidence, she thought. A man sat two seats before her bellowing a drinking song. He was well dressed, but he reeked of spirits and trouble. He had already tried to strike up contact with the other passengers around him. He was harmless, but she nonetheless hoped he wouldn't turn and begin with some kind of nonsense. She didn't know what she would do. She was in a dangerous mood. The entire day, she had wondered what was between Karin and Hopstock. She didn't want to use his first name, not even in her thoughts. What was it about him that Karin couldn't mention on the telephone? She wanted to know, but at the same time she didn't.

To her horror, Sofie saw that the drunk man was getting off at the same bus stop. She walked to the back of the bus to avoid exiting through the same door. I lack courage, thought Sofie. Is there anything more dismal than this? To feel that you've lost your self-respect in encountering others who've already done so.

Karin stood to give her a hug. A bit coldly, which wasn't strange, considering she was fifteen minutes late.

'Your hair smells like rain.'

'It began to pour just now.'

Sofie put her hands into her hair and shook it, before removing her jacket and hanging it across the back of the chair.

'What a beautiful dress you're wearing,' she said looking at Karin. 'Such a nice, warm colour.'

'Thank you. It would probably look very nice on you.'

'Except that I never wear yellow. Not any more.'

Sofie could see that Karin took the barb. The dress was wheat-yellow, a touch darker than her hair. As she sat back down on the sofa, she was like a piece of straw bent in the middle. Her height, her elegance. She was someone who people noticed when she entered a room. Sofie had always enjoyed looking at Karin.

The menus were lowered onto the table, large scraps of paper with sinuous script, almost indecipherable.

'I think I'll have wild salmon.'

'That would be good . . . But should we really polish off the remaining salmon colonies?'

Karin rolled her eyes. 'Must you always be so politically correct?'

The conversation thus far had a familiar tone. They ordered wild salmon. There weren't many others in the restaurant. Four women at one table laughed quietly and clinked with their silverware, just across from them one young and one older man sat bowed over their coffee cups. The room was circular and airy, illuminated from above by an enormous glass cupola. The stormy sky made the light hard and grey. Around them were mirrors and glass. Sofie rubbed her arms quickly, as though she was freezing. Her bracelets jingled. They were the thin, enamel bracelets that were sold in the museum gift shop, Sofie had combined several of various colours. Karin nodded in recognition.

'That's chic.'

Sofie had put on as many of them as she could find, to camouflage the bite. She hid her arms under the table. The meeting from earlier in the day filled her. The impossibility of it. The sprawling figure on the stairs, with fingers hard as claws, it was as though they were still clenched around her hands.

'I bear greetings from work. Everyone is wondering how it's going with the Frankenstein of Tøyen.'

'I don't think Otto would like it if that name gets spread around.'

'No, you're probably right about that. Does he look dreadful?'

'Well, he may not want to show his face outside for a while. But his head is working. Can you just imagine Otto sitting and staring at the wall for several days?'

Karin grinned. The waiter returned with a bottle of white wine and a cooler. His movements were agile. The wine glimmered pale green. Karin

SEVEN DAYS IN AUGUST

grasped the stem of the glass with her slender fingers. Her nails were always manicured. Sofie straightened her bracelets and lifted her glass.

'So then, cheers,' said Karin. 'It's much too seldom that I have you to myself. But that's the price one has to pay when your friend suddenly becomes your boss.'

Cheeky, thought Sofie. That sharp elegance for which Karin was known and respected.

The restaurant had become dimmer. Outdoors, a constriction. The new storm looming.

'What was it that you wanted to speak with me about?'

'Lasse Hopstock.'

'Hopstock. Do you know him?'

'You can be certain I do. I went to him for a period. You aren't planning on starting therapy with him, are you?'

'He would like it if I did.'

Sofie told her about the dinner party, the tablemate from hell, his flirtations, how he had declared divorce at the dining table. Otto was right, it was a terrific story to tell.

'And yesterday he looked me up at work, to ask pardon. And after delivering his apology, he gave me this and encouraged me to get some help.'

Sofie pulled out his card from her jacket pocket and handed it to Karin.

'Good God.'

The food arrived at the table. The salmon was almost aglow in the dark room. Barley, a root-vegetable puree, fennel.

'This looks delicious.'

'Eat, and I'll tell you my Hopstock story,' said Karin. 'It's not quite as good as yours, but it's vulgar enough.'

'I didn't have any idea that you went to therapy?'

Karin ploughed her fork into the small barley pyramid.

'Let's just say I've worn out a number of therapists. The conclusion is always the same—that I struggle with my most intimate relationships. All of my beaus, for example. Several of them are gay. So that's me. I've had many lovers too, it's not that. But I've always been a bit . . . undecided. You look completely appalled, Sofie. I didn't mean to unload all of my issues on you. It's just that I was concerned to see you together with that man yesterday.'

She pointed down at the plate with her fork.

'Oh, taste that. The salmon is excellent.'

Sofie picked at the food. Her ears were buzzing. Was the noise external, was it the rain? What was it that Karin was actually saying? They used to be close friends, they used to tell each other everything. Or had it only been she, Sofie, who had talked? She could feel her legs beginning to shake weakly. She carefully set down her knife and fork and placed her hands on her thighs. Only for a moment, and then she picked up her napkin and dabbed at her mouth. Lately, she'd felt as though her memory was full of holes. Could it be that Karin had talked about this before? Or had she always held back, kept the important things to herself? Karin was concentrated on the food. She was somehow able to speak and eat at the same time.

'Well, I started going to Hopstock, that was four to five years ago, and among other things we talked about my inability to fall in love, something that he must have taken as a challenge. I found him to be very aggressive in our conversations, so I stopped going to see him. And that was when it began. Because he took that as a signal from me.'

'A signal?'

'Yes, the fact that we were no longer doctor and patient meant that we could now start to meet as, well, man and woman, I think that's how he probably perceived it. He sent me text messages, called, came to my door . . . '

'You're joking.'

'No. And at first I tried being polite, but that just makes yourself even more desirable, you see? In the end, I threatened to report him. Then he finally backed off. I have to confess that I had quite a fright when I saw you together with him yesterday. What an unbelievable coincidence.'

Karin picked up the card that had been lying between them and tore it in half. And then she tore the halves into even smaller bits and sprinkled them across the leftover bits of food that remained on the plate.

'Just admit it. You were tempted to contact him. To try out an hour of therapy. See if he really was so bad.'

'Never.'

'Certainly, I would bet on it. That's how things work.'

Their glasses were refilled. The waiter asked if they were satisfied. Karin waved him away impatiently.

'You've talked about it in the past, Sofie. That you would like to start seeing a psychologist. But you've always put it off.'

'I've never lacked opportunities, you know that. Crisis counsellors, bereavement support groups, meeting with other survivors . . . I tried those for a while, but I wasn't able to accept the help. All the collective grief made me feel nauseous, and people had such strong opinions about how I should deal with it. All I had to do was to simply live through the grief. It was so pure, so easy to understand.'

Were Karin's eyes getting wet? That's not what Sofie wanted. Karin shouldn't cry her tears. She tried shifting to a lighter tone.

'But now I've started wondering. I've been given some signals . . . and I wonder whether I am no longer able to see things clearly.'

Karin looked at her in earnest.

'You could just try. I've said it before, you have to let out your anger. You've held too much of it inside. You are too bleak. There are a lot of people who think so. And your mother, your sister . . . you shouldn't push people away.'

The waiter came to clear away the plates, and Karin went to the washroom. Sofie felt lost as the small pieces of business card vanished from sight. She hadn't seriously considered consulting Hopstock, yet she hadn't been opposed to carrying his card in her pocket. A safeguard, he'd said. She hugged her arm. Warmth. It now felt swollen up to her shoulder. There wasn't anything visible, but there was some kind of pressure from inside, turmoil throughout her body. That's how things work, she thought. Her old doubt resurfaced again, and she knew that she wouldn't do it now either. Go to therapy in order to attain a tolerable distance to her life? No, she'd certainly had enough of staring deeply into herself. Karin returned and scribbled the name and telephone numbers of a few psychologists on a piece of paper. Sofie sat watching her, trying to sort out what had been said. *There are a lot of people who think so*. The sentence spun around. She couldn't remember telling Karin about her arguments with her mother and sister. Again, this feeling that she could no longer trust her memory, or her own experience of the situation.

The waiter asked whether they would like dessert. Everything had been cleared away, the table cloth a smooth expanse between them. Sofie felt seasick. She only ordered black coffee.

'Oh, Sofie, I'm so glad that you've decided to do this. I've been so worried about you lately,' said Karin, handing her the paper.

Here it comes, thought Sofie.

'It's difficult to say this, and I really hadn't intended to talk about these kinds of things today. But the thing is that people are a little . . . afraid of you, because you have this aura of, what should I say, glorified sorrow, about you.'

An aura of glorified sorrow.

'It makes you inaccessible, can you understand that?'

Sofie shook her head slowly. She understood, but she didn't agree with the premise. Couldn't accept the words. Such artificial labels.

'As long as the employees keep treating you like a saint, the atmosphere won't be very good. People are stiff, distant. I believe it bothers you as well. That's why I've tried interacting with you the way that I would with any other supervisor. But it may be that you think . . . that you feel . . . I'm worried that you might believe I'm working against you.'

'Strange,' said Sofie, and Karin quickly stopped speaking. 'It's like hearing Otto talk.'

A confused expression crossed Karin's face. 'How so?'

Sofie looked past her. 'I don't know. I just felt a kind of déjà vu. As though we've had this conversation before.'

'I'm sorry if I've gone too far. It was stupid of me. To invite you here, and then to nag you about work . . . '

'It's fine, Karin. Just fine. It was helpful to hear.'

Sofie rose. She remained standing, grasping the edge of the table.

'Are you ill?'

'I only stood too quickly. Excuse me, I need to go to the washroom.'

Sofie could feel Karin's eyes on her back as she walked through the glass doors and up the marble stairs. She could hear her thoughts. *There she goes, gliding away in that mystical manner of hers, the woman in black. Like a kind of nymph or elf, too good for this world.* She stood in the washroom, staring at the tiles, gleaming, white and cleanly scoured. The smell of powerful disinfectant. Everything seemed, of a sudden, so unreal to her. It was as though she was able, for a brief moment, to see through the delusion, the curious illusion that is life. She could see that she was not Sofie, that Karin was not Karin, that they were both playing at a game without meaning, without end. The sensation was so strong that it frightened her. The water circling in the toilet bowl, she was in the pipes. On the way down. She threw up.

When Sofie returned to the table, she had to use both hands to lift the tiny coffee cup. She felt empty and limp. Her blood had been siphoned out of her and was somewhere else, streaming through some other body, a real body, a warm, living body. Karin's gaze rested for too long upon her, it pressed heavily against her collarbone, like a physical weight. She had said what it was she wanted, but what was it that Karin actually wanted? Sofie turned and looked for the waiter.

Karin leant forward.

'You don't have an easy job. I don't envy you at all! There are so many people who think that they know best. And it's impossible to animate a stick in the mud, no matter what you do. But don't let it discourage you. Remember that there are a lot of people at the museum who like you.'

And then they were busy with paying. Afterwards, they stood for a while in the reception area. She endured it all. The usual parting salutations. A cold gust of wind rushed in each time the doorway opened. Outside, the cars floated above the streets. Karin waited with her for the taxi Sofie had called, the wind pulled at her dress. The yellow colour was no longer warm, but looked garish against the marble walls in the sharp light. Sofie told Karin that she could leave, she didn't need to wait. And then the taxi arrived, and both dashed off into the rain.

Otto had cheated and turned on the television, he hadn't been expecting Sofie home so early. She didn't say anything at first, simply walked right past him into the kitchen. He watched as she pulled out a drawer and took out a bag of crisps, which she began eating directly from the bag.

'Oh, I thought you went out to eat. Weren't you at a restaurant?'

'The portions were small.'

'Did something happen?'

Sofie pulled herself together, poured the crisps into a bowl and brought it into the living room.

'What do you mean?'

'You look so pale. In fact, you look awful.'

'I feel awful. I just got wet, maybe I'm catching a cold.'

She plopped down on the chair in front of him, continued downing the crisps as she stared at the TV. It was a documentary about an African human rights advocate. The commentator's voice flowed like a dark, calm river. Otto could feel his pulse sink back to normal. It couldn't be what he had suspected. It was wrong to believe the worst about people.

'Was there anything in particular that Karin wanted?' he asked carefully. He could feel himself losing his footing, although he was lying down. His fall on the stairs was beginning to plague him in other ways. The physical pains were still there, in his head, his ribs, in his smashed lips. But the fall itself, which he could not remember experiencing, had become fixed in his body. His body recalled it for him. The sensation of weightlessness. Of falling and not knowing when the fall will end. At this very moment, it was like sitting in an aeroplane that kept plunging into pockets of air.

'Oh, it's a long story. I almost have to go back and start by telling you that our friend, Dr Hopstock, showed up at the museum yesterday.'

'Lasse Hopstock? At the museum?'

'Just before I received the call from the ER. That's why I forgot to tell you about it.'

Sofie recounted the unexpected visit at the museum, and told Karin's Hopstock story.

'So this is why Karin insisted on meeting you?'

'That's what she said, in any case. She wanted to warn me about Hopstock.'

'But you didn't want to listen to her?'

Sofie looked at him, confused.

'Yes, no . . . I've actually been thinking about going to therapy lately. But I'm not going to go to *him*. Karin recommended a few other psychologists. She's apparently had good experiences with therapy.'

'Oh?'

'Yes, she told me this evening that she's been going to therapy for several years, and to many different therapists. And I found that so odd, because she's never mentioned it before.'

Otto lay staring straight ahead, eyes narrowed.

'What are you thinking?'

What was he thinking? He was thinking that life was so many things, but that it was first and foremost complicated. Everything was woven so tightly together. He was thinking that he was becoming an old man. He was thinking that life was a fall. That anything at all could happen during the few seconds that it takes to fall through the air.

'I agree with you that it's odd.'

That wasn't really what he was thinking. But it was all that he could say.

WEDNESDAY

She saw it at once, but without really seeing it. It was too unexpected, too brutal.

Light flooding the inner courtyard, and the severed branches. Luminous yellow-white patches. Sofie paused inside the gate and had to stand, unmoving for a while before she began to take in what had happened. The birches in the courtyard had been cut down. The trunks remained, halved, with a few partly chopped branches protruding from them. The trees were no longer trees but sculptures. Beneath them was a scattering of green-yellow leaves and sawdust. Sticks and twigs were strewn outward. The rest was gone. The green canopy. The boughs and foliage that filtered light, that transformed the courtyard into a sheltered chamber, that rustled in the wind, formed colours and movement. Now, Sofie looked past the damaged trunks and branches and directly at the white adjacent building, a bicycle shed and a peeling wall. She made a sound. A trembling sound, almost like a chirp. She walked stiffly towards the entry door, was surprised that the key fit, was surprised that her feet carried her all the way up the stairs. Each time that the stairwell passed a window, the new view pierced her eyes. Concrete and glass, untidy balconies, a clothesline she'd never before seen in the neighbouring courtyard. And the rigid birch spikes poking helplessly in every direction. At the last outcropping before their floor, she saw that the sky was completely open; where it had once shimmered green throughout the entire summer, there was now only a harsh light glaring through the glass. Sofie locked herself indoors, dropped her purse and shopping bag to the floor, walked into the living room with her shoes and jacket still on. Otto peered up at her from the sofa. His face still unrecognizable, a mosaic, a colour chart.

'Hi, are you home already? I must have been sleeping.'

Sofie could only stand there.

Otto was able to prop himself up so that his back rested against the pillows.

'Sofie, say something. What is it?'

'The birches . . . '

'Oh, the birches. It was a terrible riot out there, no quiet at all. So when they were finally finished, I merely fell asleep. Did it turn out very ugly?'

'There's nothing left. Nothing! They can't do something like that! Who decided this?'

'The housing association board, I assume.'

'But why haven't we . . . ?'

'We weren't at the meeting, though. We received a referendum from the board right before the summer began. Didn't it say something there, about pruning . . . '

He stopped as he noticed her outpouring of tears. Her face was set and white as plaster. The tears dripped onto the collar of her jacket, ran down her neck. Sofie stood as though frozen, her hands hanging straight down. It seemed as though she'd stopped breathing.

'Sofie. Sofie, calm down. Sit down. Do you hear me? Sit down on the chair there.'

But Sofie didn't sit down, she sank into the floor where she stood, sank together into a crumpled pile on the floor. The pile issued a few deep sobs, which turned into raspy wailing. Otto gathered his sore body and stood up from the sofa. A flashing in his head, he doubled over for a moment. Then he hobbled to her and tried to take off Sofie's jacket. When that didn't work, he squatted down and put his arms around her. She was still crying, but more subdued, into her jacket lining. When he wasn't able to calm her down with physical contact, Otto went in search of tissue. He returned with two napkins that he jabbed at her. Her hair, he tried pushing it out of her face, gathering it in his hands. It had become wet and tangled. Sofie held the napkins in front of her face and continued sobbing.

He didn't have much to say by way of comfort. The birches had been badly mishandled, he could see that too. Although they would most likely grow out again, have new shoots and turn green once more, they would never be as fine as they had been before. But there wasn't much they could have done. The neighbours below them had been complaining about the lack of light for several years. Hadn't Sofie noticed?

'You would never have been able to prevent it, my dear. In the end, it was only us up at the top who wanted to keep the birches. And soon they would have covered us in shade as well. Just think how much they've grown since we moved here.'

He stroked her head. Her weeping episode was beginning to ebb. Soon there was only an occasional whimper.

'They were the only fresh and healthy things in the entire neighbourhood.'

'They will grow back. There were people from the parks department here, they know what they're doing.'

Sofie turned, and Otto thought she was going to sit up. But instead she stretched out her legs and lay down completely. Otto had to release her hair, and her head slid below the table. Most of her body rested atop the Persian carpet that they had received from her parents when they moved to Tøyen. Her eyes were clasped shut, her face was swollen.

'Get up, Sofie. My dear, you can't lie like that.'

She didn't answer, only pulled her jacket more tightly around herself. Otto sighed and struggled to his feet. He fetched a blanket and lay it over her. On his way to the washroom, he noticed her shopping bag in the hall. There was a stab in his ribs as he bent down to pick it up. She had bought an organic chicken breast, cream, fresh pasta. He put the food away in the refrigerator and returned to the sofa. There was a cosy little impression left by his body.

It was completely silent, apart from Sofie's jagged breath. Otto lay staring up at the ceiling. Black dots danced before his eyes. The rather lovely expression 'seeing stars' is, rather, more akin to flakes of falling ash in one's eyes. In the past few days, he'd had an ample amount of time to study the surrounding room. The stucco work, a beautiful frame for the case in which they'd buried their lives. The thought scared him. But this wasn't how they'd imagined life would be. They had had two children, they had had so much life around them. And now Marie was dead and Peter had settled down on the other side of the planet. He and Sofie did their best to draw meaning for themselves. A different type of life. A type of harmony. Viewed in this way, he could understand Sofie. That she was beside herself because of the birches. He lay an arm over his eyes. Was taken aback as his parents emerged from the darkness. Side by side in those white lacquered coffins. Black soil. Dark and still. He pictured them to himself as mummies, anything else was unthinkable. He bore only warm feelings for them, a warmth that was nearly painful. His mother had died suddenly of a particularly aggressive cancer. His father's grief was just as abrupt, he had died a few months later. Heart failure. It was a

219

shock for his father to be alone all at once. His parents had puttered around one another for their entire lives, but Otto had never thought of it as love. Shared dreams, coexistence, habit, care. There were many words he could use for them, but perhaps love was the only correct one? He wondered what it was that Peter saw when he, very rarely, was together with him and Sofie. Certainly not the image that they believed they projected, of two people fulfilling one another, uplifting one another. Perhaps he felt sorry for them? Perhaps he thought they were pathetic? It was hard to know with Peter. He hadn't been at Marie's funeral. It was a long journey, it was expensive, he'd had to take an exam that he had postponed. It had been wrong of them not to insist that he come. Peter knew very little about what they had gone through. But he had also suffered the loss. What might Peter think about it nowadays?

Otto sensed a weak movement beneath the table, a sniff. He shouldn't pester, but he had to try prodding her up soon. My wife is lying under the table, he thought. With her shoes on.

The light was no longer so harsh. Otto folded his hands across his stomach, which responded with a loud rumble. The black dots were nearly gone. The walls. The artwork on the walls. Some had been inherited, others had been purchased by Sofie. He fixed his gaze on two lithographs. Images that made Otto uneasy, although he liked them. Motifs from Rosmersholm, illuminated faces and dark doors, he stared at them until everything shifted to fields of darkness and light. A stream swept him along, objects in the room began to swirl. Books and paper, lamps and art and chairs, everything swept up in the flow. It's not dangerous as long as my eyes are shut, he thought. And suddenly, a sound in the other room. Sofie was no longer lying on the floor, she was standing out in the library letting down the blinds. It was the doorway out to the balcony, the one facing the courtyard. The light no longer streamed freely through the room. Otto lay still and blinked.

'What are you doing?'

After a while she responded. 'Shutting the blinds. I never, never want to look outside again.'

'Have you completely snapped? We can't keep the blinds down all the time!'

'Can't we?'

She rushed past him, out into the kitchen. He could hear her opening a bottle of wine. She returned to the living room and stood at the dining table. A book lay there, opened, with a yellow highlighter in the fold between the pages. She took a sip of wine. An anchor. Earth and iron. She read aloud from the paragraph which he had highlighted.

'I did not know then how much was ended . . .' She began to read.

'I did not know then how much was ended. When I look back now from this high hill of my old age, I can still see the butchered women and children lying heaped and scattered . . . all along the crooked gulch . . . as plain as when I saw them with eyes still young. And I can see that something else died there in the bloody mud, and was buried in the . . . the blizzard. A people's dream died there. It was a beautiful dream.'

She looked up from the book.

'I thought you'd forbidden me to read. And yet you sit here with this!'

'I couldn't get through more than two pages. After that I had to go lie down.'

She ran her hand over the page of the book. A citation from the Native American, Nicholas Black Elk. And nothing had changed in all the time since.

Otto struggled painfully to sit up on the sofa. It hurt to breathe, and his head was like a kettle boiling. He looked at his wife, the image flickered before his eyes, she was out of focus. She stood there at the table, so rigidly, so accusingly. What was she accusing him of?

'It's so little, the thing that stands between us and the horror. A thin sheet. But people don't understand it. How crucial beauty is.'

Otto blinked several times. He did understand it. But how could he let her know?

'So, when the birches are cut down, you experience it as though the horror is coming closer.'

She nodded. 'It's about losing terrain. Each day we lose terrain. Everything that has been beautiful, will become defiled.'

She stood there. A woman with a wine glass. Long, sleek hair. A woman without a face. The light was so unusual. Outside, the sky had turned an iridescent, pale grey shade, like the inside of a shell. She waited.

'I understand you, Sofie. We think a bit differently, but I understand you.'

'No, you don't. You think that there will be justice, that as many as possible should get what they want. The same amount of light for everybody, it's all the same if beauty vanishes.'

'You're reducing the matter.'

'No, on the contrary. I'm opening it.'

Otto ruffled his hair, which was sticking straight up from earlier. When he put his glasses on his nose, he looked completely insane.

'I think that I need a glass of wine as well.'

He was given half a glass.

'Now I'm ready to discuss it,' she said.

'Discuss what?'

'Moving.'

He coughed, wiped his mouth carefully with the back of his hand.

'That may be a bit hasty, don't you think?'

'You've been talking about moving to Kampen, up to the heights. Let's find ourselves a small house with a tree in the garden that we can do with as we wish.'

Sofie sent him a challenging look, fully aware that she was on thin ice.

'Well, what do you say?'

'This comes as a bit of a surprise, as I'm sure you're aware. You've never been willing to discuss it before. And now you suddenly think it's a good idea. I never know what you're thinking.'

She sank her gaze. 'Well, to be honest, I've never thought of it until just this moment.'

'So how seriously should I take this discussion?'

She took the empty glass out to the kitchen. Otto put both hands over his face, but resisted the urge to rub. It was too painful. He could barely recognize his face any more. His skin was bulging and warm, it stung and pricked everywhere. Move again? Well, they never thought they would be here for the rest of their lives. A tiny little cottage would be nice. He could get his own house, Sofie her own tree. He pictured a child's drawing that he must have once composed, of their house at home. A square with small squares for windows. A staircase, a crooked door. Drawn crookedly to look askew. Three stick figures and a ball with four legs stood next to the house. Mother, father, child, dog. A tree with a green circle on top. The car was not much larger than the dog. The thin, green line upon which everything balanced, was the lawn. Always freshly mowed. The thin, blue line up above was the sky. Most of the area in between was white. Empty space.

'What are you thinking about?' Sofie had seated herself in the chair across from him. She had been to the washroom to rinse off, had gathered her hair into a ponytail, put on a light T-shirt. She looked much better.

'About a little house at Kampen. With a garden. And a tall fence around it.'

'And lilacs.'

'Anything that you want, Sofie.'

Her eyes filled again. Clear, twinkling. They brimmed over. Wet spots on her T-shirt. He could hear himself that his voice was tired, toneless: 'Isn't this about more than the birches?'

The birches, their whispers. The green canopy below the sky.

'It's about the birches,' she said softly.

There was a flash of lightning. He counted the seconds, waited for the thunder. It didn't come. So the storm was still far off. He wished it would never come. Or that it would come soon, so they could be finished with it. They were never finished with it. He remembered her rage during the memorial service. Black, boiling oil. A rage without limit. That's how it started. Many people had said fine words, the right words. But there had of course also been words that were completely wrong. What could you expect from people in that situation, only two days after the catastrophe? But it continued. The rage over everyone who tried to interpret the incident, to own the grief. He could share her feeling somewhat. Those fine words which had given strength at first, but which eventually stopped working. Which became the mantra that anyone at all might use for anything at all. *More freedom, more openness, more democracy*. As Sofie once put it: The roses withered and turned to vainglory. Norway, that tiny country triumphing over evil and hatred. The Rose Parade, the photos were spread throughout the world. Hate and madness against a wide river of love. It was sensational, nearly unbelievable. Was this strategy truly possible? The first rose parade was unifying, strengthening. The next was a joke. People pulled out some old environmental protection ballad, walked through the streets singing about a heaven full of stars. More love, more sentimentality, more roses and 'blue ocean as far as the eye can see'. What became of the rage? Sofie, who stood at the edge of the abyss, could only see how black it was, could only see how empty. They need comfort too, Otto had told her. They are doing it to comfort themselves, they must be allowed to do it. It was like trying to mediate between heaven and hell. After that, she had declined all invitations to groups and gatherings, all attempts by other survivors to contact her, declined any support or offers for help. She has been too resolute, thought Otto. She has turned her back, in mistrust and contempt. Mistrust of the authorities, of everyone who was responsible and said that they acted responsibly, but who failed in the crucial moment. He could understand her up to this point.

But hadn't she also turned her back on other people, even those closest to her, who couldn't understand and follow her? Wasn't it only a question of time until she would turn her back on him as well?

His mobile phone lit up, and then a jaunty ringtone. When he answered, Sofie could hear from his voice who it was, and felt throughout her body that there was something she'd forgotten. She had forgotten Peter. Otto looked at her as he spoke. She squirmed.

'Oh really?' said Otto. 'I haven't heard anything about that.'

Sofie stood and walked out to the kitchen. What should she say? She couldn't admit that she'd forgotten to tell Otto about her conversation with Peter. That would be fatal. She would say that she had postponed the conversation in order to tell him when he had recovered somewhat. The phone conversation lasted for a good while. She cleaned as she listened. And then it was quiet in the living room. She walked out into the doorway.

'Why didn't you tell me that Peter had called?'

'I was the one who called, while you were sleeping. And then . . . then I thought I should wait to tell you, until you'd recovered.'

'But that was two days ago!'

'I thought he sounded upset. But I might have misunderstood. It was dumb of me, I'm sorry.'

'You plain forgot!'

'No, like I said, I wanted to wait a bit, until you were yourself again.'

'You are standing there lying. Can't you just say it like it is? That you forgot! You never mention anything, you just drift around, it's impossible to know what you are up to!'

Sofie reluctantly met his wide eyes. They looked like they could pop out of his eyes at any moment. He looked like he wanted to grab her. So couldn't he just do it? Grab her by the ponytail and drag her through the room. Otto, who was always so calm that everyone else felt flustered in comparison. Always so pious. Pious, pious, pious. The word filled her, but she kept it in. It rang in her ears.

'It's not enough to just go asking pardon afterward. You don't tell me what you're thinking, even if it's something that concerns me, or us. You receive important information that you don't deliver. You are completely up in the clouds. It's like shouting into an empty, dark sack. I called your doctor today . . . '

'What? You called my doctor?'

' . . . to check whether you'd really made an appointment on Friday, like you had said. And you hadn't.'

Her eyes flickered.

'Maybe it was on Monday . . . '

'No! Stop! You had better fucking give it a rest now, Sofie!'

Otto grabbed his wine glass and flung it at full strength. Sofie felt the air pressure as it blazed past her temple, and a small splatter across her neck as the glass hit the wall. A tinkling sound. She looked at Otto, who sat panting heavily. His gaze was fixed on a point behind her. Slowly she turned, and saw red wine running in stripes down the wall.

They spoke in hushed voices. A sort of indifference had come over them, more frightening than the fury that had preceded it. Sofie picked up the largest shards of glass and dried up the wine. She couldn't quite expunge the red stripes on the wall.

'Damn it,' she mumbled, scouring with the cloth and cleaning powder. 'Now it will be harder to sell the flat.'

'We'll describe it as an artist residence. That way people will expect flecks of red wine here and there.'

Otto was exhausted, he had reclined on his back. Sofie rose and picked out a few small bits of glass that had landed in the chair. They left behind small, red spots.

'Come, sit down.'

'Yes, I'm just going to finish here. There's still glass everywhere.'

'That can wait. Come, I want to talk with you.'

Sofie put down the cleaning powder and cloth and positioned herself on the outer edge of the sofa. Folded her hands in her lap.

'Here I am.'

He kept his eyes shut, wasn't certain whether the rattling noise was coming from his head or down below on the street. He fumbled around for her hand, clasped it.

'Perhaps it was rather excessive of me to call your doctor, but I'm worried about you. You're trying to get out of it. Being evasive.'

'Fine.' Sofie's voice was cold. 'Fine. I'll go see my doctor about the tick bite.'

He opened his eyes. 'So it *is* a tick bite?'

'I believe so. But I'm not really certain.'

'Didn't you deny that it was a tick?'

'I never denied it. I said that I didn't know what it was. You say that I don't tell you anything, but you're not particularly good at listening either. It swelled up, and I saw that there was something inside the sore. It only got bad after I tried to pick it out.'

'So you knew, the entire time, that it might be a tick. Without admitting it, without doing anything about it. You know there's been talk about an epidemic, a new virus, people are getting really sick.'

'The papers always exaggerate.'

'One might think you had a death wish!'

A powerful blast of wind gushed abruptly through an open window, and a flower pot fell to the floor. It was as though someone was trying to break it. Just come, thought Sofie. But she stood up to shut the window and had to take a large step over the broken pot. The naked flower roots stuck out from the clump of earth like small, white worms.

'I think about her too,' he said. 'Every single day.'

'I know that.'

Sofie remained at the window, looking out. Tiny, sharp flashes of lightning cut above the ridges to the west.

'I think about her as she was. The way she would shuffle through the room. A bit happy and a bit sad. A pup who hadn't yet found her place. And when she would finally sit down, the way she would always mess with her hair. I most often picture her in that white jumper, the one that your mother knitted.'

'Judit. It was Judit who knitted that.'

'Every day I wonder what she would have done today.'

Sorrow is something that can only be shared for a short while. After that, everyone continues to live alone in their grief. Sofie looked at her arm. What had happened with her arm? It was no longer lovely. She had grown too thin. Her small moles had become darker. And Otto talked. Talked and talked. There was never enough talk.

'I can understand about the photographs, that you don't want to have photos of her around, that you don't want her old things around. I can understand all of that. You would rather have a living, and more unclear picture of Marie inside of you than a photo on the wall reminding you that everything stopped there. Which would remind you, each time you would look at it, that it will never be supplemented with graduation photos, wedding photos, photos of the first grandchild. There are many people who consider that a strange line of thinking, but I can see the logic in it.'

He sees the logic in it, thought Sofie. But he has a photograph in his office. Like a hidden treasure. Maybe Otto would prefer to have photos hanging at home. She thought about what Karin had said. *Glorified sorrow*. Were they afraid of her, everyone? Everyone except for Karin? What kind of person had her sorrow made her to be? She searched for something to say.

'I can no longer see her for myself. I was able to for a period. When I looked at her friends, I could see her. But now they are university students, they are so grown up! Some of them are doctors by now. It's impossible to picture her now.'

'Is that why you're considering going to therapy now?'

'That, and for several other reasons. I'm forgetting things. Imagining things. People look at me strangely. I think I'm starting to go mad.'

He looked at her earnestly.

'You are pretty mad for not going to the doctor with that tick bite, in any case.'

The blinds swayed slowly although the windows were all shut. They could hear the thunder breaking in the distance.

'You have to promise to go early tomorrow. Do you promise, Sofie?'

She shook his hand on it. He held on.

'There was something I read today. About how one must have an eye that permits transformation. If not, the world will only get smaller and smaller around us. This is what you are thinking about, isn't it?'

'An eye that permits transformation.'

'Yes.'

'Otto,' she said. 'That is a lovely thought.'

Sofie had to make herself a strong cup of coffee before she began cooking. She stood at the counter and blew on the scalding coffee, impatient to imbibe. Then she had the idea to pour in some milk. And a bit of sugar. She had drunk two glasses of wine on an empty stomach. Not surprising that she felt dizzy. But that strange prickling along her right jaw? She pressed on the bone, a numb feeling. A bit like earlier, on her arm. It was probably a good idea to go to the urgent care. Then she would have it done with. The cup of coffee and cream formed a small pool of warmth in her stomach. She found renewed strength. She stood for a long time looking into the refrigerator, unsure what exactly it was she was after. She shut the fridge door and instead slanted open the window. The wind pulled at the window suddenly, tried prying it from her hands. The papers on the refrigerator flapped, a calendar fell on the floor behind her. There was nothing else for her to do but to shut it. But where was the rain? Both the city and the fjord were nearly blotted out by a consuming, violet hue.

The door to the pub that was often open was now shut. But outside, Poor Dog lay in his usual spot. Otto had talked about setting the dog free. He had planned it, how he would go out and liberate the poor creature, lead him away, bring him up to their flat. What would happen after that, his thoughts about that weren't nearly as clear. Sofie had mentioned it wasn't certain that the dog *wished* to be set free. Maybe he would prefer to stay with his owner, regardless of how badly he was treated. Couldn't she have taken Otto seriously, supported him? They always had to analyse, evaluate and think everything through so thoroughly. In the end, it was impossible to follow through. *An eye that permits transformation.* She could be standing here now, explaining to the tiny dark-haired child on her arm, pointing and babbling. A warm, soft body, a newly bathed child with clean clothes. And Poor Dog could come padding in to eat out of his dish, that happy crunching, tail wagging.

Two men stumbled out of the pub throwing punches at each other. One of them could barely stand up, he reeled and swung punches into the empty air. The other delivered a kick to his side so that he fell on his face. Now the pub owner had come to the door and stood, pointing, chiding. The man who had kicked the other, lurched down the street and disappeared. The one lying there on his stomach, floundered helplessly with his arms, as though going through a dry-run for swimming. His trousers had slid down, stopping far down on his rump. Poor Dog sat watchfully, observing with his ears pressed flat on his head. The pub owner helped the man to his feet and supported him into the pub again.

This was so far away from her childhood garden in Bestum. Where the wind made the trees rustle and stoop. But now all of the flowers would be struck flat, first by the wind, and then by the rain. She heard a ding. Now, two, both her phone and Otto's in the living room. The message was from Karin, who had sent her an evening photo from her balcony, with a stunningly colourful sky above the city. *The sky suddenly turned blood red. Have a good stormy night!* From Karin. Sofie wanted to answer, but couldn't think of anything to say. Should she respond with another quotation from Munch? Write 'a good evening to you'? She was incapable of delivering fixed phrases and small talk. She had been allergic to it for eight years. She couldn't even bring herself to say 'Thanks, I'm fine' when people asked how she was doing. Even if they asked with that look in their eyes that implied you should best respond that things are fine. Because nothing else would be acceptable. Nothing else can be endured—for those who ask. So then, what should one respond, when you've lost your daughter and the only thing you desire is to be struck by cancer or some other illness that can wipe you out as quickly as possible? Sofie had learnt to respond: 'I have my ups and downs'. Everyone has their ups and downs. Oh, yes. She had been so angry at Otto because he always responded the way that everyone expected and wanted to hear, that things were going well with them. On the phone, at parties, when people asked: how are things going? Speak for yourself! she had screamed at him after one dinner party. Things *are* not going well, they *have* never gone well, they are *never* going to go well, so would you please just shut up? If you say one more time that things are going well with us—with *us*— I'm going to leave you!

They'd had so many sick arguments. They, who only wanted the best for each other. Who only had one another. A life without Otto was unthinkable. She could also never imagine for herself that they would live in another place. The problem was that she had difficulties imagining a future at all. It had been that way for a while. One day at a time. Draw strength from what she could. *The will to live when the best days have gone.* She had read that once, and held onto it for strength. Such courage had been hers. Had it not? Sofie sank down on to one of the two stools at the kitchen table. She thought about what Otto had said. An eye open for transformation. It was up to her now. She shut her eyes. She pictured green grass. A garden. That was her in the beautiful garden, in a floral summer dress. Barefoot in the grass. Was the garden in Bestum? Was it a small, yet unknown garden in Kampen? In any case, there were lilacs. She recognized the scent of them. Purple, plump, aromatic clusters of flowers. Otto was seated beneath a tree reading a book. She tried to picture a house. It must be white. There must be old-fashioned stone steps in the front. Peter sat on the steps. T-shirt, brown, strong arms. A child's laughter. He was following her with his eyes, the tiny girl bounding about the garden. Her hair stood out like a cloud behind her. Peter called for her to be careful. Not so fast! he called. Otto looked up and smiled. He had got older. He looked like a grandfather.

Otto woke, heard only the wind. Everything was dark except for the kitchen. So, she must still be cooking. He stretched out for his mobile phone, to check the time. He sighed when he read the message from Karin. Was she trying to lure him out again? Then he noticed that the time was nearly ten thirty. He scrambled to sit up.

'Sofie?' he said tentatively. There was no answer. A pounding in his chest. At once he knew it for certain. She was gone. She had gone, out into the storm. She had understood everything, even the things that he didn't understand. She had had enough. Otto stood up slowly. He took the trouble to fold the blanket. He pushed his wrinkled shirt tail down into his trousers. He picked up the book that lay opened on the table, and replaced it on the bookshelf. Finally, he walked with stiff steps over towards the kitchen. And there she sat. At the tall kitchen table, with her head propped on one hand. It looked as though she was half asleep with her eyes opened. In front of her was a cup half-filled with coffee.

'Sofie, my dear.'

She came to herself, lifted her head. Her gaze turned slowly towards him.

'Oh, hi.'

'Were you sleeping?'

'No, I don't think so.'

'It's ten thirty! And you haven't begun cooking?'

'Ten thirty?' She looked around in wonder. The counters were clean and tidy, the oven empty and cold. The darkness pressed up against the window, had crept up on her without her noticing it. She met his eyes, afraid.

'Then maybe I did sleep a bit after all?'

Otto walked over and felt her hands, which were cold. Hugged her head in towards his stomach, she let it rest there.

'The sorrow has regrouped,' she mumbled into his shirt. 'So now we must, as well.'

'Oh?'

She's been dreaming, he thought. 'And here I thought that you had gone your own way,' he said, his voice thick.

'Gone my way?'

'I woke up and it was completely silent, and it was very late and I thought you had left.'

'I am not going to leave you, my husband.'

He put his hand under her chin, raised it up and looked down into those dark eyes, large in her narrow, pale face.

'No matter what happens?'

She nodded mutely.

I have to tell her, he thought. This nonsense with Karin, it must be brought to light. Sofie has to know about it, she must have the chance to evaluate the situation. Otherwise, Karin can keep attacking him from two sides. His heart raced. This was a new thought for him. Karin as an external enemy, himself a repentant sinner. He kissed Sofie's forehead. She shut her eyes. When he released her, she turned her head towards the window.

'The rain hasn't begun yet.'

'No, it's only the wind.'

'But it has to come?'

'It will come soon.'

It will have to be during the dinner, he thought. We can't talk about this until we've put something in our bellies. He walked over to the refrigerator, took out what he had placed inside earlier that evening. It felt as though that had been days ago, not hours. Behind him he could hear her standing up and turning on the oven.

'I can do it,' she said.

She began to dress the chicken fillet with herbs and cheese. He put the water on for the pasta and tugged lightly on her ponytail.

'Then I'll set the table.'

Sofie didn't wait for the oven to heat up, but placed the chicken in and started cleaning old food out of the fridge. She had to do something to try to repress her hunger. How in the world could it be so late already? She was on her way down the stairs with two full garbage bags when she remembered about the birches again. Her stomach clenched. I will never get used to it, she thought, although she knew that she would. She had to press open the outer door, and as soon as she was outside, the wind took hold of the bags, making them behave like two unruly children halting and pulling on her. She walked sideways to avoid looking at the stripped birches. On the shed roof, something loose banged in the wind. As she lifted up the garbage cover to dump in the bags, a bolt of lightning flashed and lit up the inside of the shed. The thunder boomed in almost the same second. A sharp, ringing sound, like a mountain splitting. But still no rain. Sofie walked slowly back up the stairs as she held onto the railing. She had felt so strange when Otto came into the kitchen and she realized that she had been sitting there for so long without doing anything. The feeling still remained. One hour, completely gone.

Otto was standing at one of the windows.

'Come look. Things are really starting to happen out there.'

She stood next to him. The wind came in waves. They looked directly across at the new, half-finished blockhouse. The Grove. The plastic, anything loose, flapped. A wheelbarrow that lay at the top of one of the concrete modules, inched slowly towards the edge. Sofie thought she could almost hear the scraping sound. The wind grabbed hold of it and tipped the wheelbarrow over the edge. It fell, vanished, and they heard a car alarm going off. And just after that, two more car alarms. Howling, unsynchronized sounds penetrating walls and windows. The facades on the opposite side of the street were illuminated by red and yellow flashing lights. Sofie looked at the hoisting crane, imagined it fall, severing their courtyard in two. A flash of lightning lit up the entire street, it looked like daylight outside, it lasted for several seconds. Thunder followed directly after, and then the lights went out. A gigantic hand had flipped the switch for the whole city. There wasn't a single visible light. Blackness inside and out, everything melted into one until another flash of lightning lit up, revealing that there was in fact a city out there.

'Are you afraid?'

'A little.'

He put his arms around her. She pressed her face into his chest. They rocked back and forth.

They pull out their chairs in unison. Otto's gaze glides over the basket of toast, the ancient platter with the fillet of chicken in its juices, the large ceramic bowl with steaming, flat bands of pasta. The electricity is back on, but he has taken out two large, weighted silver candlesticks that they bought together, long ago, at an antique dealer in Paris. Only the light from these two candles falls across their meal. The green glasses look nearly black in this light, the colour of a dark pine forest. Sofie unfolds the paper napkin and lays it in her lap. She has always liked evenings in August, the few days and weeks that it is still summertime and warm, but dark enough to kindle a living light. The light flickers for a moment, painting shadows across the wall. Moving shadows, beautiful and eerie at the same time. She stops, tilts her head.

'Hush. Is that the rain?'

Transformed to shadows, they both appear as giants.